A new **ABC**
Wellness, Mindfulne

New York
to
NEW YOU

THE (31/7) ODYSSEY

Dear Diwakar,
With best wishes & compliments!

Manoj Gupta :

MANOJ GUPTA

First Edition: July 2020
Printed in India

Printed at Dhote Offset Printer, Mumbai
Typeset in Garamond

ISBN: 978-93-88698-56-6

Cover Design: Prashant Gopal Gurav
Book Layout: Yogesh Desai

STORYMIRROR
Stories that reflect you

Publisher: StoryMirror Infotech Pvt. Ltd.
                145, First Floor, Powai Plaza, Hiranandani Gardens, Powai,
                Mumbai - 400076, India

Web: https://storymirror.com
Facebook: https://facebook.com/storymirror
Twitter: https://twitter.com/story_mirror
Instagram: https://instagram.com/storymirror

DEDICATION

To my family: Mamta, Harshita, and Yajat
You are the most important parts of my life.

And

To my parents Om Prakash and Sushila
for setting the foundation on
which this book is based

ACKNOWLEDGEMENT

First and foremost, my praise and thanksgiving go to the Divine; for His blessings, inspiration and thoughts during my writing sessions at 5am, where I found my energy levels in absolute harmony with the cosmic energy.

Any accomplishment requires the efforts of many people and this work is no exception. I especially thank my wife, whose patience and support was instrumental in realizing this task. I thank my daughter for being my companion, my son for his flawless inputs, and my brother for his continued encouragement during the writing process. I am extremely grateful to my parents, for setting the foundation on which this book is based.

I am grateful to all of those with whom I have had the pleasure of working during this project. I thank every member of the publishing house who has provided me extensive professional guidance along the way.

My heartfelt thanks also go to those who have contributed to this work, even if anonymously.

I would also like to profess my deepest gratitude to Vedic literature, the teachings of which are eternal. They brought a paradigm shift in my outlook towards life.

Finally, thanks to the Niagara Falls and the Angel for the inspiration behind the cover page. It represents creativity flowing continuously within us, something that is ever rejuvenating and energising - the indissoluble nature of this book.

PREFACE

Some journeys are best enjoyed solo. Especially the Outside-In - the journey, where you travel from the outermost layer of your Physical personality to your Soul within. Pleasures in life come from discovering places however, best pleasures are derived by rediscovering yourself deep within.

The book New York To New You is an attempt to put a prime focus on *reality* over *relative reality*.

- *Reality* is always you and the infinite power you are carrying inside.
- *Reality* spreads positivity, whereas *relative reality* spreads anxiety.
- *Reality* pushes you to go beyond obvious, whereas *relative reality* tries to bind you within the defined periphery.
- *Reality* brings joy, whereas *relative reality* always keeps searching for a ray of happiness.

I remember day when I first experienced Déjà vu. Until that period of my life, it was just a French word for me meaning experiencing some event, which has not happened. I was amazed to know more details about the topic. Digging deep inside into the topic, some unknown territory was opening like a deck of cards. I don't remember how many books I started reading and doing research from, but every time I came across a new philosophical concept, mostly misinterpreted by modern science, it challenged my logical mind. Through that process, I read many books, ancient scriptures of various religions, interpretation by scholars and philosophers. The more I started learning, the more I was getting submerged in the deep power of science and metaphysics within me. Broadly and vaguely, metaphysics addresses fundamental questions about the nature of reality.

Even though we are the custodian of many powerful elements in our life, we barely get glimpse of all those until our death. Psychologists, philosophers and mythologists might have a different connotation of our inner self, and this personality within us makes us what we are today. Awareness about inner self makes our journey more meaningful and pleasant and dissociates us from depression, trauma and frustration - which are a result of feeling lonely and isolated in the time of problems. When we realize that we are never alone, never short of helping hand, happiness is the only payoff.

The book is the outcome of all that research & reflection spanned across two decades and a recollection of various experiences documented in tranquillity.

My joy knew no bounds, when the draft manuscript got appreciation from someone who used to write speeches for one of the powerful Prime Ministers of India and was the Editor of very influential National newspaper. Some of the early readers of my manuscript co-related this book with the summarized wisdom of several hundred books and a few even started finding changes in their life through this book.

I hope this book brings similar experiences in your life.

This book is all about you and your Odyssey within.

This book talks about two men on two opposite sides of the world brought together by a moment of serendipity. James, an investment banker and darling of Wall Street in New York. The other, a Guru, the Life Transformer from India.

- One who believes in 'my way or the highway', the other who thinks that the real expressway of life lies within.
- One who cannot control his emotions, the other who can actually read them.
- One who has made bad choices; the other who helps to make the right choices.
- One lacks discipline, the other has mastered it over time.

And then there is a mysterious character RK who has a mystifying link with both these characters.

What happens when the three meets after a flight from New York?

This book tells you that the *New You* lies within you. All we need is to realize it. The book focusses on human engineering, which is overlooked through the various education systems of the world and tries to explain the concentric layers of human engineering with practical examples and implementation methodology.

How to read this book
This book needs to be read slowly and one chapter at a time. The principles in this book are eternal and universal. They are applicable in your personal, social and professional life. This book is about enhancing your mindfulness, wellness

and inner leadership.

This book explains the distinction between *How to make a Living* versus *How to Live*. How to make a Living is part of life, but not Life. Take this book as a life manual.

The book has characters, drama, story and suspense — but above all, it has a message, including *'how to'* steps to transform your thinking, and in turn, your life.

Material success is just a part of life, but not Life!

I recommend after every chapter or after every two chapters, you should take a pause and write down if you are able to co-relate something from your life. You can write down your feelings in the blank pages provided in this book. I strongly believe, after you are done with the last page of the book, you will have discovered a different you, which is a more powerful you, than you know about...

Manoj Gupta
London, UK
https://www.manojgupta.com

PRAISES FOR THE BOOK

Really enjoyed reading the book. As a man of faith, I believe in self-improvement and reliance on higher power. The book opened my eyes to new ways of thinking about my faith. I thank the Author Manoj Gupta for that. I like the way the he has interwoven a story with the concepts that he is teaching – it is an effective literary device. Thank you for sharing such a personal and powerful book.

Norm Merritt
CEO, Qualitest Group

This book is a bold step towards defining human engineering in an environment that is dominated by business and science. Manoj has smartly captured the ancient principles that help us understand how we can be successful without compromising our inner peace and satisfaction.

Dharmender Kapoor,
CEO & MD, Birlasoft Limited

This is a very engaging book, full of distilled wisdom, presented in a warm and personal manner. Every reader will discover a nugget that will elevate their life. Written for people who want to define what really matters, it will not only expand your thinking - but also transform your life. Reading and following its advice and insight might well be the greatest present you can give to yourself, your family, friends and business colleagues. Thank you, Manoj, for this great book.

Hugo Pluess,
CIO & Executive Board Member, Imperial International

There is so much one can take from this book. It is full of smart and straightforward ideas which come together to form something very special. But more than anything 'New York to New You' describes an experience, which people in the fast lane will often dream of; this book certainly fills a void.

Yaron Kottlar,
COO, Qualitest Group

The book teaches you simple techniques to help discover and explore oneself and 'how to live' in harmony with the external world, no matter what one is going through inside or outside. The book is written as a simple story that each of us can associate to very easily and can be very useful if put into practice with discipline.

Shankar Narayanan
President & Global Head, Tata Consultancy Services (TCS)

This is a fantastic, very well written book. I love the way incidents and experiences are shared.

Reading this book made me unlearn and relearn ABCD of my life, so many thanks. While reading I was trying to relate the book with everything happening in the world; COVID19, lockdown, stock exchange meltdown. It is very relevant in the current times and going forward.

Looks like Manoj's 100th book, it is written so well.

Rangarajan Raghavan
Former CEO & MD, HCL Infosystems

Most of us know 'how to make a living' but only a few know 'how to live' ...and live a wholesome life. The profundity of this subject has been narrated through an interesting conversation between two extraordinary characters. 'New York to New You' is a playbook that has the potential to transform you and unleash your fullest potential, if you imbibe the key messages.

Rajeev Sawhney
Former President HCL Technologies,
Chairman - Zokyo Ltd

I must say Manoj is a brilliant writer - the book provides an important tool in refocusing my mind and energies, at a time in my life where self-awareness has never been more important. A very enjoyable read, once you start, it becomes hard to take a pause. The language is tasteful and engages you with the story; never a dull moment. This book is a definite read for everyone.

Sameer Nigam,
CEO Stratbeans Consulting

Fantastic! This book is a must read for all those who want to live their life to the fullest. The corporate world can be maddening, and this book offers great insights on how to lead a more meaningful and stress-free life. The idea of striking balance with your inner self and the external world is well explained with real life examples. The book is a helpful guide to anyone wanting to understand core tenets to living in harmony with oneself.

Avadhesh Dixit,
CHRO, Acuity Knowledge Partners

Manoj has truly written a book for the times. All around the world you see people seeking external solutions to real or imaginary problems they have, while the solution often lies within them. Consider this book as the GPS to find your direction - in this case the destination happens to be deep inside yourself to unlock the best you!

Apurva Chamaria
CRO RateGain, Best-Selling Author

A fascinating and gripping story of how everyday complexities and inevitable failures of a professional's life can be resolved using simple spiritual but powerful tools. Manoj has succeeded in explaining simply and effectively, the complex concepts of abstract thoughts spelt out in the Upanishads, as solutions to problems that nearly all young executives of our time face.

A must read for all the professionals who are burning candle at both ends.

Ashok Mishra
Entrepreneur & Author

New York to New You is an amazing book as it relates our lives very well with the spiritual world and human engineering. In day to day life, we have somewhat lost 'the human' from mankind and have forgotten that we are not here to be unhappy or anxious. The book, based on the conversation of two primary characters, focuses on many essential elements of human engineering, which I could relate so much to my own life. I really admire the thoughtfulness of the Manoj Gupta, delving deeper into the life we are living in this present world. So, if you are looking for a change in your life, then you should read this book 'New York to New You'."

Abhishek Agarwal,
CEO, Consummate Technologies

If you think life is moving too fast to take control of, or if you are stuck in a corporate rat race as a cog in the wheel - Manoj's 'New York to New You' will prove to be a gem for you. This book will give you the tools to understand 'who' you actually are, and the limitless things you can achieve. When I started reading this book, I thought I'd finish it in parts and in a week. But it was a Sunday morning when I started reading it and just couldn't put it down. It is a must-read for anyone looking to empower themselves through self-awareness and self-help.

Atal Malviya,
CEO Spark10, Author

NOTES

NOTES

CONTENTS

PROLOGUE

The atmosphere was tense in New York's Wall Street and mystery was in the air! A prominent, extremely successful investment banker had vanished from a hospital - into thin air. With successful investments of almost five billion dollars, the news of his disappearance was trending all over the social media platforms and business channels.

#WhereAreYouJamesHatman and #JamesStopHiding were some of the leading hashtags on Twitter and other platforms. As if that was not enough, the paparazzi were having a field day out there on the morning news, gunning him down, especially the clamorous and raucous news anchor of channel News 365 - Arnold Gosling. He was hell bent on ripping James Hatman to shreds.

The debate continued, "Well, we all have heard the expression, 'pulling a rabbit out of the hat'. If you want to see that in the corporate world, you have to meet James Hatman. This highflying, global investment banker has generated wealth from stocks that no one thought possible. He has literally created rivers of wealth from seas of deserts. Just how much wealth are we talking about? Five billion dollars to be specific. It's astounding how the man invested his time, money and efforts into sick industries, companies and stocks that were in ICU mode, and now are alive and kicking like never before."

Another analyst piped in, "Yes, Arnold, Mr Hatman's achievements are indeed remarkable. From turning companies barely surviving, to extremely thriving, this man could do no wrong in the financial world. He plays all the right cards making him a financial wizard. He moves the pawns, horses and bishops on the chessboard achieving checkmates with the queen moving in for the kill. This man is the grandmaster of the financial world. He strides like a behemoth across the financial chessboard."

The news presenter shot back, "Though I think he is a tad over ambitious, ravenous and will consistently play it 'my way or the highway'. That's one of the reasons several trading professional bodies, including the US Treasury, have trained their eagle eyes on him."

The business analyst interrupted, "Maybe he should be given the benefit of the doubt. After all, at such a tender age, he has accomplished what others only dream of. He will become seasoned with experience and with the harnessing of the market dynamics. Most of the successful people out there have gone for the kill when the situation demanded it. Hatman is no different."

The news presenter countered, "Ok, maybe we can give him the benefit of the doubt, but how can you explain his absence from the meeting of Neo Industries, a project he was personally involved in? I guess things have gotten a bit too personal as rumours are rife about Hatman's recent breakup with his supermodel girlfriend, Eliza. A relationship as volatile as the stock market. We have watched with fascination the graph of their relationship go up and down through the years. Has Neo forgotten the thin line which dictates business and pleasure should be kept apart? Or has Hatman realised that Neo Industries does not have the required engine for growth? After all, the company was about to file for bankruptcy."

24 hours ago

Switching on the light in his room, the man realized he was in a hospital suite. He looked frail and mentally broken. It had been extremely hard for him to handle all the negative limelight focused on him. As he reached for his smartphone, Dr Riya Soni quickly grabbed it and switched it off.

She said, "Mr Hatman, please relax. The paparazzi are out to hunt you down, even though you are in this precarious state."

He said, "Tell me something new Doctor."

Dr Soni was smiling and thought that the man's sense of humour and resilience had remained intact.

"You know Dr Soni, life is all about timing, whether it's a Formula One driver who gains pole position with a few microseconds, or a cricketer, in your part of the world, hitting a six." Dr. Soni raised her eyebrows. "Yes, though I am American I am aware of cricket and Sachin Tendulkar." James continued "I love... his straight drives. Sadly, my timing was all wrong today. My emotions got the better of me and I completely mis-timed the test drive of the new prototype of Neo cars. The engineering team had warned me about the test drive, yet I took the risk of driving it with none other than the Founder of the company. Look at the result! I am in hospital; the Founder is dead and Neo car's dream lies in the ICU."

"Mr Hatman, it was an accident, don't be so hard on yourself. You can't always predict these things."

"I guess the line between confidence and overconfidence

is obscure. I did not realize when I overstepped it. My career has been a great ride so far, unfortunately when I needed to slow down, I couldn't, and now my future hangs in the balance. The accident happened exactly on the same day I was supposed to present to the world, the amazing security and safety features of this car."

While the two were talking, James' secretary had entered the room unnoticed, and was listening intently. She interrupted the verbal proceedings, "Mr Hatman, what you really need now is a safe and sound night of sleep. I will take care of all that's happening outside the four walls of this suite."

"Dr Soni, that's Emily, my secretary. She always has perfect timing and knows what's best for me. I guess she is right, as always. Time for me to say nighty night."

Once they left, James was engulfed by a killing, smothering silence. He was too afraid to close his eyes as the terrifying flashbacks of the accident kept returning non-stop. His thoughts were running riot: If it hadn't been for this accident in the Neo car, he would, at this moment have been at headquarters presenting his vision for the company, mesmerising the stalwarts of the automobile industry. His strike rate in presentations was almost a 100%, ensuring he would always get the nod for any new business or venture, whichever pitch he walked on to. He had believed this would be no different. After all, he had a new revolutionary technology that would take, not just the industry by storm, but also bring a smile on the faces of environmentalists around the world. Alas, if only his life could make a U-turn!

Knowing he had no respite of a U-turn; he went into flashback mode to the conversations he had had with the mentor of his engineering student days.

Though James was an automobile engineer he lived in conflict between his emotions and scientific reasoning. He would debate for hours with his mentor and with his peers.

It was at one of his college lectures that he had started a one on one session with his professor.

"Professor, you said - Passion is everything. Always follow your passion."

The professor replied, "That's right, but right now you are getting too passionate about this subject. Look James, passion and practicality need to have the right balance just like a weighing scale. That's because both complement rather than compete with each other. Tell me James, why do we have cars?"

"Simple. To take you from point A to point B."

"Good. So, why do we have these fast cars or supercars and Formula One cars?"

"To help us reach faster to a particular destination."

"James, what is your definition of 'faster' for cars?"

"I don't get you professor!"

"Ok, let me rephrase the question, what should be the maximum speed limit for vehicles?"

"That's a difficult one professor. As humans, we would love to drive or travel at max speed but it's not possible due to many factors like infrastructure, climate, roads and the habitats we live in."

"Exactly James, you have hit the nail on the head. That's precisely why we don't use rockets on land to travel, as it may result in human error and disastrous accidents due to the sheer speed of the rockets. We might have a great passion for rockets but we recognise that their optimal use is in space and not on earth. That's where the delicate balance of passion and practicality come into play."

James was listening raptly.

The professor continued, "Let me give you another car example. Imagine, with passionate dedication you have created the finest petrol engine in the world. Various auto industries have queued up outside your office to buy this engine for their upcoming cars. Customers buy the cars and absolutely love the new driving performance. Then, one day, a customer threatens to sue you as his car has broken down after filling fuel at a petrol station. This creates news all over but soon you discover that the customer is an idiot or at fault."

James asks, "How is that possible professor?"

"The silly man filled diesel instead of petrol in his engine. The fact of the matter is that you crafted the finest *petrol* engine in the world which, however, is impractical on *diesel*. The customer should have known that. The biggest learning for you is that *passion* should also fuel *practicality*."

"Son, a great idea is not in the mind. It is one that comes to life. I have seen plenty die in my lifetime. Great ideas are like a great basketball team on paper. Unless that team on paper executes their plans on court, they continue to be a great team, just on paper."

"Passion and practicality have always gone hand in hand in human evolution. Man had the passion to explore and travel. Therefore he invented the wheel. We wanted to hunt animals for food, therefore we came up with weapons."

A pensive James paused, looked up at his professor and said, "That's why they call people like you mentors and people like me rookies!"

"Come on James, you are far better than a rookie, I am proud of you."

James shook the nostalgia from his head and thought: 'I have failed you sir. Today I would have loved your precious words of advice'.

Suddenly, he heard a loud commotion just outside his door.

"I need to see Mr Hatman right now, it is super urgent or else he could get into deep shit," said an agitated voice.

"I am sorry sir; he is resting and doctors have banned visitors. It won't be possible for you to meet him today."

"Every minute you waste gets Mr Hatman deeper into a serious legal mess."

James recognised that voice at once. It was Jordan Jackson, popularly known as JJ - his legal counsel. His voice was laced thick with angst and frustration.

James requested the nurse to let him in as it seemed that something urgent was afoot.

JJ was all apologetic as he told James, "Look, James, I know you are in the hospital and you need rest but I have bad news and more bad news."

"There we go, another piece of bad timing coming my way," James murmured to himself.

James fixed eyes on JJ as he said, "We have lived through tougher battles JJ. Tell me what this is about."

JJ handed him a piece of paper and told him that this was the bad news. As soon as he opened up the document, James felt he had been hit with another concussion just like the one he received from the car accident.

"Who could have done this?" A furious James looked at JJ for an answer.

JJ looked straight into the eyes of James and said, "Your girlfriend and there's some more bad news I was talking to you about."

"You got to be kidding me," James was now all but hysterical.

"I am not, and here's proof of it."

JJ showed James a message from Eliza, which read:

'Sorry James, it ain't working for us anymore. I think this relationship was a big mistake. I have to pay the price for it now. I have to be a government witness for your stupid mistakes. I don't want to spend the rest of my life in prison like you. Goodbye James, adieu.'

"Bitch, how could she do this to me?" James yelled.

Shaking off his anger he looked at JJ and asked, "What are my options now?"

"Now do exactly as I say," JJ told him.

Within a week this story became a flashpoint in the business media and community. Not only was the Neo Industries crisis growing, there was no sign of James Hatman. 'Where in the world is he'? everyone kept speculating.

Somewhere on the other side of the world, in India, it was dawn as a man woke up, and was scrolling on his mobile phone, watching the news of his own disappearance. He was eagerly waiting for someone who, he hoped, had all the right answers.

CHAPTER 1
The greatest piece of engineering

It was 5:30 am. The first rays of the morning sun were breaking through the dark billows of clouds. It was a bright sign of equanimity and hope trying to make its way through the clouds of uncertainty. That feeling resonated among the hundreds of people gathered, as they do every morning at the Anand Ashram near Triveni Ghat, close to the River Ganges, popularly known in India as the 'Ganga'. The people were always on-the-dot, on time. Come what may.

Geographically, the Ganga is a river that flows from the Himalayas down to the Bay of Bengal for a whopping distance of 2,525 km. That is mere statistics. For Hindus, it is thousands of years of tradition, heritage and culture flowing in every wave and drop of the river. The river, over thousands of years, has witnessed millions of stories along its banks; seen motley empires change hands and has been a pivot for several religions and civilizations. And speaking of stories, the origin of the Ganga is just as fascinating as its significance in human history.

It is said that the powerful and divine King, Bhagirath, prayed for years and practised austerity (Tapasya in the Hindi language) to please the Gods and the heavens. Such was his devout way of life and virtuous dedication that none other than

Lord Shiva (one of the supreme Gods of Hindus) decided to gift him with the holy river – the Ganga. This would flow from the locks on his head onto the gorges and valleys of the Himalayan range which is also known as the abode of Lord Shiva. It is believed that Lord Shiva and Bhagirath spoke for a mere seven minutes but by the time the King returned to his realm, aeons had passed, seven generations to be specific. Thus, many believe that Einstein's Theory of Relativity was first discovered in India, thousands of years ago.

The Ganga is mythical, magical and miraculous. But it is not just mythology or religion. Ganga's science continues to turn the heads of the scientific community and baffles them to this day. After all, how would one explain that the Ganga continues to have 25 times more oxygen than any other river in the world? Store water from this river or consume it even after years, it hardly loses its essence or taste. You normally have a filtration plant beside a river body to cleanse it but for some inexplicable reason, the Ganga continues to self-cleanse itself. That explains why it is considered to be a holy river or why, in the hope of attaining nirvana, after cremation, the ashes of people are immersed in it.

Speaking of immersion, the people waiting at the Ashram were immersed in anticipation of the Guruji who was soon to arrive. Suddenly there was a voice in the crowd, "Guruji, will soon be here to shower us with his blessings."

At the Ashram, every male follower or devotee was denoted as 'Guru Bhai' while every female follower was called 'Guru Mata'.

Later in the day, special evening prayers were planned for the full moon night. It was not just the evening or the Ashram that would be special, a special guest was about to grace the occasion today.

"Don't go by Guruji's ordinary attire, he is a man who possesses extraordinary vision, ideas and approaches towards life," one of the Guru Bhais informed James who was looking around in expectation.

James was quick to reply, "Really? What makes you say that?"

"You might mistake him for just another self-proclaimed spiritual Guru but this man enjoys the best of both worlds - science and spirituality". Guru Bhai was now enjoying the attention his words had elicited.

James enquired, "And, what makes you say that?"

Guru Bhai replied, "Not many know this but Guruji graduated from the globally renowned Indian Institute of Technology, Mumbai. In those days, it was called IIT, Bombay. That's not all. He has done his Masters in Physics from Cambridge University and even has earned a double PhD from MIT in Metaphysics and Quantum mechanics."

James eyes nearly popped out of his head and his mouth hung wide open. He was dumbfounded, to say the least. Regaining composure, he retorted, "Sorry but what is he doing here in an Ashram when he should be up there on some stage of a TedX show. Wonder, what's the point of earning all those degrees when you end up doing something that's one-eighty degrees in the opposite direction? In another world, this man could be earning millions."

Guru Bhai had a twinkle in his eyes and a smile on his face as he replied, "Now, that's a capitalistic and industrialistic mindset talking. My friend, humans went through evolution to create machines, not to become one. Sadly, that's what it has come to, in this day and age. Are we realizing our true human potential? We are stuck in the daily rat race of accumulating wealth or paying our next loan or mortgage instalment. Is this really what we are meant for, as the human race? There is definitely some reason we are the most advanced species on the planet. This Guruji, with his seamless blend of science, art and spirituality, shows us the path to aligning our minds and bodies so that we realize our true potential."

Suddenly the entire room was filled with a divine aura. Such was the effect of the mere presence of Guru Manvik. He softly made his way to the front of the hall to address his audience. All eyes were fixed on him as though he had cast some magical spell on the people in the room. This included James. On this cold gloomy winter morning, Guruji's entrance seemed like warm sunshine, melting the hearts of all the people in the room.

Guruji was peace personified. His zen-like state of mind and enigmatic smile sent waves of positive vibes and energy throughout the room, resulting in the rapture of his devotees.

While everyone was wearing layers of protective clothing against the winter chill, Guruji was draped in just a thin layer of cotton. Probably, it was his inner bliss and benevolence that added the extra layers of warmth to his body.

There was also great warmth and cordiality in his voice as he started talking. "Good morning friends, it's wonderful to see you all here under one roof. Looking at all of you, I feel you are asking yourselves a question: what am I doing in this early morning chill, listening to a Guru?' Great! I love your thinking and it's excellent to have questions in your mind. After all, human evolution took place thanks to some very pertinent questions like: why is the earth round, why did the apple fall on the ground. Is it possible to fly like a bird? Can I go one day to the moon? If no one had asked these questions, we would still be in the Stone Age. So why not start this session with a question? Here we go, it's a very simple one. According to you, what's the greatest piece of engineering on planet earth?"

"This little thing," said one voice as he took out his latest iPhone from his pocket.

James quipped: "I think it's the aeroplane on which I flew and made it to this event, Guruji. Without it, globalization, travel and tourism would not have been possible."

Guruji looked at him, smiled and asked, "By the way, how was your flight?"

"Everyone had a little smile on their faces." I think it's got to be the computer and the internet, a geeky looking man stood up and answered.

"You Googled me, didn't you?" the Guru riposted.

James thought that the guy did have a sense of humour in his armour of spirituality.

Guruji said, "Your list will go on, some will say TV, others will say the telephone while the younger bunch here will also say Netflix." Now the crowd had a good ha-ha moment.

"Do you notice something in all these answers? Most of them are mere objects. That is the tragedy of human evolution. Today we have objectified everything. Be it brands or applications on our smart devices. We have forgotten how to live life holistically. We are all busy with how to make a living but very few of us understand *how to live life* as it was meant to be. Coming back to the question, all of you were wrong. The greatest piece of engineering is sitting right among us."

James was perplexed and so were the other people in the audience as they looked at each other. "The piece of

13

engineering I am talking about is you," he pointed to a man in the crowd. And then he began pointing towards random people in the hall and kept saying you, you and you.

"My friends, each one of us is the greatest piece of engineering ever built. After all, where on earth would you find a body that has the perfect amalgamation of physical, emotional, intellectual and spiritual processes occurring 24/7? If you are not the best piece of engineering, what is? I believe the world is not just 24/7, it's **31/7**."

Everyone in the audience had a startled look on their faces. All had the same question in their minds. 'What the hell is 31/7'?

CHAPTER 2
The 31/7 of Human Engineering

"That's exactly why I would like to discuss a topic very close to my heart but before that I would like to know what is going on in your minds," Guruji said.

A few hands went up in an instant. Suddenly, there came a volley of questions fired at him.

- "If humans are the best piece of engineering then why do we suffer with anxiety and sorrow?"
- "If I do not focus on how to *make a living*, then *how would I live* ?"
- "Mind over matter – what does it mean in human engineering?"
- "I know anger is not a good emotion yet I cannot control it. How do I master it?"
- "Can we attain control over our minds and bodies?"
- "What is more important - mind or body? How can both work in one continuum?"

The Guru was all eyes and ears to their questions. Then suddenly he raised his arms, a signal for everyone to stop. There was pin-drop silence with all eyes pinned on him. There was an air of anticipation in the room that was almost tangible. With a smile illuminating his face, the Guruji began:

"My friends all those questions have answers which I will uncover in the topic called 'Human Engineering'."

Being an engineer himself, James was wondering what the hell this topic was.

'Just some more spiritual jargon I think. Such a term as 'human engineering' does not even exist but then what are these people in this audience doing'? James mused.

James looked into the audience. It was a random mix. But it comprised prominent researchers, scholars and scientists from all walks of life and from all over the globe.

It included:

- A delegation from Germany which was researching the string theory;
- A team of scientific experts from Switzerland who was recently involved in the Higgs Boson particle or the 'God particle' experiment;
- A team of NASA experts exploring Interstellar travel possibilities and
- A hodge podge of people from different parts of the country.

James wondered why and how such a distinguished and varied audience was here to listen to Guruji. A disciple got up; he was called Rishi Parth. He announced, "Before we go further, I request you all to close your eyes and breathe in and breathe out for the next two minutes. Forget everything else and just concentrate on your breath."

James felt extremely thwarted and it's skeptical and so he went into his monologue mode.

'What am I doing here'?

'What's the point of getting into this breathing mode'?

'Why not get straight to the point about human

engineering'?

'This feels like a complete waste of time'.

Just then, the Guru Bhai noticed the skeptical look on the face of James and gestured for him to keep his eyes closed.

Now Guruji took over, "Hope you are realizing the sensation and vibrations from the environment and the people around you. Now please gently open your eyes.

"Just as in a restaurant you need an enticing ambience to relish the food, so too you need the right vibe and awareness levels to have a profound understanding of any topic.

"Can a car run on only four wheels? No, right? It is made up of gears, pistons, steering wheel and many other parts. These *constituents* come together to offer you the best mileage and driving experience. It also needs roads and by-lanes to be driven around, which is termed as its' *field of operation*.

"Similarly, human engineering comprises *constituents* and *fields of operation* to offer you maximum personality mileage as an individual."

He drew a chart to show 31 *constituents* and *fields of operation:*

- 5 organs of perception – eyes, ears, nose, tongue and skin;
- 5 organs of action – hands, feet, speech, generative organs and organ of defecation;
- 5 sense objects – object of senses corresponding to five senses of perception. Sight for eyes, sound for ears, smell for nose, taste for tongue, and touch for skin;
- 5 great elements – air, water, fire, earth and space. These are the five fundamental elements that constitute the world;
- Mind – which produces impulses, feelings and

emotions;
- Intellect – which thinks, reasons, judges, decides;
- Ego – which arrogates feelings and thoughts to oneself;
- Kernel - the seed of individuality;
- Unmanifest – refers to Soul, Atman and
- 6 subtle constituents – desire, hatred, pleasure, pain, intelligence and resolve.

These 31 *constituents* create seven personality layers of us humans. Guruji then drew another chart:
- Physical– comprises organs of perception and action;
- Emotional– comprises the mind and its attributes - desire, hatred, pleasure and pain;
- Intellectual– comprises the intellect and its attributes - intelligence and firmness;
- Ego;
- Memory;
- Kernel, the seed layer and
- Soul, the unmanifest

The five Sense objects and the five Great elements are termed as *fields of operation.*

The Guru looked into the eyes of the audience. He saw many flummoxed while a few were yawning, including James. The Guru turned towards him and said:

"I can see that this topic is getting too heavy for your mind. Ok, let me ask you about something that you love – that's eating. What's your name?" He looked straight at James.

"James," he said loudly.

"Ok James, what's the best part of the cake except for the cream and cherry on the top?" James could visualize the cake on his girlfriend's last birthday which had layers of chocolate and cream.

He replied, "The layers."

"Bang-on James, I am impressed."

The Guru, now looking at the audience said, "Human engineering is nothing more than various concentric layers coming together to offer you the finest pleasures of life and the taste of happiness and success."

James found the analogy highly appetizing. He agreed: this man can talk.

Guruji exhibited the chart that had seven human concentric layers:

He stated, "you must be wondering what these layers are."

CHAPTER 3
Seven layers of the Rainbow

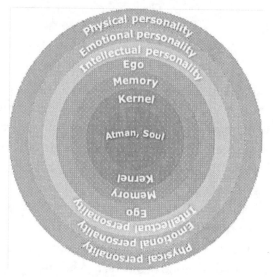

"Let's go right from the outer layer to the inner layer. The outer layer is largely made up of your *Physical* personality, the layer depicted by the red colour in the diagram which has ten key ingredients – five organs of perception and five organs of action. You can point to James and say his name, you can point at me and call me Guru or as you like." He again made it a light moment for the audience with his gift of gab and quirk.

"My physical personality is a lot about how I interact with the physical world. Right from smelling that cup of coffee to seeing a beautiful girl. Your organs of perception and organs of action have a cause and effect relationship. Imagine this, you see that beautiful girl, which makes your day."

There was a naughty smile on the faces of a lot of men out there.

Guruji continued, "What you have just done is to use your eyes, the organs of perception, which results in you going over and talking to her. That's where your organ for action comes into play as you walk to her and open your mouth to start a conversation. That is pretty much your physical personality.

"Next in line is your Emotional personality represented by the orange colour. It has five main ingredients which are your mind and its attributes comprising desire, hatred, pleasure and pain. Let's come back to that girl you saw. When you see her every day, you have a gleaming smile on your face because she arouses happiness and pleasure in you. When you talk and bond with her, your organs of perception and action get in touch with your emotions buried deep within. This is the reason why your bond with her gets stronger. In the coming weeks, months and years, you share laughter and also a tear or two. That explains why when you see her with someone else, you are a tad jealous and when someone hurts her you are in deep pain or hate the circumstances around you."

"But isn't life more than just emotions?" James raised his hand and asked.

Guruji had a smile, "That's an excellent observation, James. I can see, from getting bored initially, you are starting to enjoy this."

James was surprised that the Guru had noticed his scepticism initially and now could feel his switch to positive vibes.

Guruji continued, "Life is not just about emotions, it's a lot about making decisions, which are usually tougher than simple emotions. Emotions sometimes can get the better of you and result in wrong decision making. That's where your next layer comes in handy. Friends, that layer is your *Intellectual* personality represented by the yellow colour. This comprises three main elements: your intelligence, resolve or diligence and knowledge. Having an arsenal of these three weapons can take you places in your life. To begin with, you'll need intelligence in the form of data, analytical tools and a differentiated proposition. This needs to be backed up by hard work and diligence.

"Going a step further I would say that diligence will pay you more than intelligence. That's because people who often think they are too intelligent, many a time, try to create shortcuts, which create wrong U-turns in their lives. So, be diligent, never give up. Always show resolve in whatever you do. The third ingredient is knowledge. By this, I mean knowledge of people around you or ever-changing situations or dynamics. This will enable you to grow faster than ever before."

James was just looking at his skin and feeling his face. He had never known that he had so many layers underneath him, layers which work in tandem to make him the person he is. This was all starting to make so much sense now.

"May I ask a question?" a voice from the audience asked.

Guruji replied, "Certainly but speaking of I, it brings

me to the fourth layer. And that is I, me and myself – the Ego shown by the green colour. Well, the ego is important and can drive motivation but having too much of it leads to self-destruction. Let us think of the Great Indian epic Mahabharat where it was just Duryodhana's ego which led to the great war between the Pandavas and the Kauravas. It was Hitler's ego that had him believing he was the most powerful man in the world. This led to the deadliest war in human history, with World War II. So, always be confident but never let overconfidence get the better of you."

Guruji turned to the man who had wanted to ask a question. The man said, "Never mind Guruji, maybe later."

Guruji continued, "A while ago someone said that the greatest piece of engineering is the computer or the smartphone. What makes these devices so special? Well, it's the fact that they can multi-task and process information but more importantly, they store information in their hard drives. The fifth layer in human engineering is our hard drive, the Memory, shown by the blue layer which stores information, emotions and memories, good bad or ugly. Creating good memories results in a more positive attitude. Painful memories result in negativity and isolation. Therefore, always smile and think positive even when the going gets tough. That's how you evolve as a person."

James, in a moment of retrospection, felt all the trials and tribulations that he had undergone as an investment banker and of course in his personal relationships too. But quickly his meandering thoughts returned to Guruji who was making an important point.

"Speaking of evolution, human architecture has evolved over millions of years. We all have different abilities to think and behave when a situation presents itself. This layer is the seed of human engineering, called kernel, represented by the indigo colour in our chart. It is intrinsic and unique in each human being. It's like two children, born in the same household but one ends up as a law enforcer and the other as a lawbreaker. That's the kernel or the seed, the sixth layer in our human engineering coming into play."

James now was in admiration of the Guru who had broken up human anatomy, not into organs or tissues, but onto layers on the physical, physiological, psychological and philosophical levels.

"Last but not least, I would like to get to the core – the seventh layer. This is the subtlest layer of all. It is known by different names: *Atman*, the *Soul* or the *Spirit* of your body, denoted here by the violet colour. This is the most fascinating layer of human engineering. It remains in the un-manifested form, but manifests itself via the kernel, the seed layer. The phenomenon is akin to electricity manifesting itself via filament as light.

"In various philosophies and spiritual sciences, the *Soul* is considered to be a separate entity of the human body. It's also called the inner voice or the inner consciousness that transcends the physical body. Let me give you a simple example. Let's say, you have the finest guitar in the world. You are even great with your strings but if you can't make that audience smile, laugh and cry along with your tunes, that's just playing music, it is not soulful. The soul is what drives your deepest consciousness, emotions and feelings into energies.

"It is simple and easy to remember the rainbow colours for the seven concentric layers, from outermost to the core as an abbreviation ROYGBIV, the opposite of what we learned for the rainbow: VIBGYOR.

"Let me give you another example. What happens when you switch on a torch?"

Someone from the audience said, "We see a flash of light shining?"

"Good, and do you see a lot of colours flashing at once?"

"No, just a single colour, it's mostly white or yellow."

"Now tell me what happens when I take the same torch and pass the light through a prism?"

Guruji continued with a commanding aura, "It breaks down the white light into seven colours. So, you see the beauty - the light and the prism are two separate entities with individual characteristics till they come into contact with each other. The soul is like a torch and the kernel is like the prism. When the soul comes into contact with the kernel, manifestation happens – similar to the refraction process when the light hits the prism. The unmanifest soul, manifests via kernel into thoughts, emotions, actions and perceptions.

"So, these seven concentric layers, having the seven rainbow colours are the seven wonders of human engineering. I think this should be all for now. I know there are a great many questions and doubts in your mind but I would like to say 'hold your horses' because there's a long road to traverse in this journey called human engineering."

Rishi Parth came forward and said, "Why don't you let your thoughts digest along with some food for sustenance? Breakfast is ready. Let's meet for another insightful session after breakfast. Hope you don't snooze but come prepared with your questions. It will show how aware you were. After all, the next session is all about awareness."

'Awareness'? James murmured to himself.

"The only thing I am aware of at just this moment is the need for a steaming cup of coffee along with some spicy Indian snacks."

James loved spicy Indian food despite having a western palate. "I must have been an Indian", is what he used to say to a lot of people. Guruji overheard him as he passed by. He looked at Rishi Parth and said, "He reminds me of the rebel I once was. He will go places."

CHAPTER 4
Life is simple, why complicate?

"Wow! This is some place," James said to the Guru Bhai he had met earlier. After all, the Ashram was majestic. Both in terms of size and location. Cushioned between the Himalayan ranges with the river Ganga as its backdrop, it created a boundless flow of energy throughout the Ashram. It was a welcome relief for James. His life as an investment banker had always seen him on the move at workplaces in tall concrete jungles and five-star hotels but zero-star nature trails.

The Ashram was not just about spirituality, it provided jobs and livelihoods to several craftsmen who kept creating wonderful handicrafts using recycled components. Some of these were being exported to global markets while some were being supported by corporate social responsibility (CSR) programs. There was a school for teaching subjects that are not taught within four walls or on a blackboard. The subject was called Life. Here kids were taught *how to live,* not just *how to make a living.* A specially designed course, which was a rich mix of moral and value-based education with academics.

The more James roamed the campus of the Ashram, the more he came to the realization that there is a world beyond materialism, brands and dollars. He realized that he was rich in these three, which were about *how to make a living* but he was absolutely poor in *how to lead a life*. He was also fascinated by the Guruji's talk of this morning, where the Guruji had beautifully broken down human anatomy into seven concentric layers filled with rainbow colours using ROYBGIV as an abbreviation. He found this simile pretty novel.

Replete with food and drink, it was now time to head back to the huge central hall.

Rishi Parth welcomed everyone back and made way for the Guruji to take over.

And Guruji began, "Human engineering is mainly a lot of balance. You cannot have an empty stomach and a mind full of ideas." Everyone had a smile on their faces.

Rishi Parth again put up the chart of the human engineering seven concentric rainbow layers.

"Before I get to the subject of awareness, I would like to know if you understood the seven concentric layers of human engineering. Are there any questions?"

A few hands went up. Guruji requested them to introduce themselves, one at a time, and ask questions.

"My name is Wolfgang; I am from Germany - thank you for the insightful session of this morning. I had never known or heard of the coherence of rainbow colours with seven concentric layers of human engineering. It made a lot of sense to me. However, I still have doubts on some of the questions raised in the earlier session:

- "If humans are the best piece of engineering then why do we suffer so much anxiety and sorrow?"
- "I know anger is not a good emotion yet I cannot control it. How do I attain control over it?"

- "Mind over matter – what does it mean in human engineering?"

"These are wonderful observations Wolfgang, and sets a good context for our *Awareness session.*

"For every creation to function properly it requires a maintenance regime. I gave you the example of a car earlier this morning to explain its constituents and *fields of operation.* For the car to constantly be driven smoothly, it would require timely maintenance and servicing. Isn't it?"

Everyone nodded in agreement.

"Similarly, your personality-vehicle also requires necessary maintenance and upkeep for it to function optimally. However, most people neither know nor follow the necessary upkeep and therefore land into the zones of anxiety, anger and sorrow.

"The rainbow colour formation of the seven concentric layers is similar to a brand-new car. However, for it to remain in good shape, one needs to follow the necessary maintenance and upkeep regime.

"Similarly, the human personality-vehicle requires a simple upkeep regime of the *ABCD* to give it maximum mileage."

'*ABCD?*' James once more slipped into monologue – 'Now, what the hell is this'?

He was into a new management school, as he had never before heard jargon like 'rainbow' and '*ABCD*'.

Guruji continued – "Modern-day education systems teach you every other thing about the world, but do not cover a single dime about *You.*"

The audience was in complete sync with his words.

"In the modern education system, you are taught A for apple, B for ball and so on. That's the academic education

31

which offers you a degree to earn a living. It, however, does not focus on teaching one how to live. But Life offers meaning for your being. It has another set of *ABCD*s."

Guruji took out a chart and wrote:

A–Awareness;

B–Breathing;

C–Choices and

D–Discipline.

Now Guru Manvik looked straight into the audience and said, "that's life. As simple as that. Yet we all love to complicate it.

"Let me simplify it for you starting with *A*.

CHAPTER 5
The air of being aware

A is for Awareness

"Awareness is deeply embedded in the seven concentric layers of human engineering. Let's build a scenario to understand it: you and your friend buy tickets to New York on different flights. The destination is set. The departure date is fixed. The difference is that you have an economy class ticket and your friend has a business class ticket. Both of you are now sitting on separate flights. Your friend is sitting in business class while you are getting into the economy class. Your friend gets a welcome drink and you are still waiting for a glass of water. Now here your physical personality layer comes into play. Right from the time you enter the aircraft, you notice the smile of the air hostess to the food you are served."

James did remember his business class flight to India.

Guruji continued, "Now just imagine during the flight, there is heavy turbulence and the pilot of your friend's plane is not able to fly efficiently, which creates panic among the passengers. This is where it invokes your emotional and intellectual layers as passengers get ready for evacuation. Plus, it creates negative memories as you have a fear of dying. You must be wondering, what is the soul layer in all of this? Think of it, how would you and your friend fly in the first place if there was no aviation fuel? That is the soul of an aeroplane. Even though you take fuel for granted when you are on that aeroplane, you can't fly any class let it be first or economy."

James being a hotshot investment banker, had taken so many flights around the world, yet this thought had never occurred to him. This was a new learning curve for him, something that he hadn't learned in any Boardroom or MBA school.

"If I were to invite you to Apple's iPhone manufacturing plant, you wouldn't waste a minute thinking about whether you should go. Once you are in the factory, you'd be awestruck at the way gadgets or smart devices are manufactured these days. But have you ever considered your own body as being the greatest manufacturing plant? Every day you experience the raw materials of the five sense-objects and five elements of nature, which you receive as an intake via the organs of perception – which undergo processing with emotions, memories, ego and intellect, and resulting in output via the organs of action. Just like you need electricity for a manufacturing plant to come alive, you need the core layer Atman, the Soul to bring life to the inert human body."

'Another key learning thought', James muttered to himself. Dealing with so many technologists and people from diverse sectors, he had never ever stopped to think or imagine that his own body was the finest piece of biological, social, chemical and physical technology, all working in sync to create, innovate and evolve as a race.

Guruji continued, "This continuous cycle of raw materials, input and output continues till you ultimately cease to exist. That is why it is extremely important to be aware of the entire human engineering manufacturing plant. I will now be talking about *Awareness*.

"Let me start this with our favourite four-letter word - Love. Remember, I told you about the boy meets girl scenario this morning?"

"When you look at the girl we spoke about earlier, you feel happy and your hormones go on a roller coaster ride. That girl evokes passion, elation and positivity in you. Initially, you are too shy and coy to take action but you eventually do, and try interacting with her. This is what we call the superficial or physical layer interacting with your emotional layer. So, the two of you click and get into a relationship. Initially, you hit it off and the sparks are flying. The emotions and hormones are kicking in. As some people in the West say, 'you've got a thing going'. The feeling is so fresh and new like a pizza out of the oven with all those toppings, right?"

The crowd smiled as James wondered, 'Has this guy ever eaten a pizza'?

And then Guruji asked a thought-provoking question: "Now tell me, is this feeling enough for a long-term companionship?"

There was a resounding 'no' from the crowd.

"Human engineering goes deep down in layers. So, from your physical and emotional layer, the engineering moves next to the rationale layer or your intellect. This is the phase when the honeymoon period of the relationship is slowly fading away as you ponder the dynamics of a long-term relationship with your partner."

The audience had a grin as they heard this statement from the Guru.

He continued, "Now your head gets clouded with

questions – is this person trustworthy? Can he or she provide you with a sense of security for you and your family? Will our outlook, thought processes and aspirations align in the long run?"

James closed his eyes as he focused on his girlfriend. He was missing her terribly over the past couple of months.

"Awareness comes from things as they stand inside you. This means an analysis of your value systems, beliefs, habits, feelings and intuition. It's your internal SWOT (Strength-Weakness-Opportunity-Threat) analysis."

A number of people from the corporate world were able to relate to that term.

Rishi Parth put up a chart which elicited some relevant questions from the audience:

- Am I ready for a relationship right now?
- Will I be able to support a family at this phase of my life?
- Is this a mere fling or something more?
- Will this turn out to be like my last failed relationship?
- Love is fine but what about my finances?
- Am I ready for kids?
- My parents divorced, will my fate be the same?
- Will my family approve of him/her?
- How different is this relationship from my last one?
- How does my partner add value to my life?
- Do you love yourself?

"These are all questions that you start asking yourself rather than talking them over with your partner. I also find the last question the most fascinating. Because I have often seen people enter relationships when they are sad or emotionally empty within. They often fall into the trap that someone will come into their lives and fill this vacuum. One of the most critical aspects of self-awareness is self-contentment. If you are not happy or in love with yourself, how will you make your partner happy? It's plain and simple: if you don't have 10 dollars in your pocket, how will you promise someone else 100 dollars?"

"This is just one facet of your life. Awareness is important in every aspect of your life. The more aware you are, the more you are in control of your emotions and responses. What happens in the external world will not bother you, especially in the social media hungry world. So, the next time your friends post a selfie with their partner from the most exotic place on the planet on any social media page with the #RelationshipGoals, it will not affect you. That's because you are aware, you already know what you expect from yourself, your relationship and your partner. Maybe you should reply to your friends - #DoesNotMatter."

There was a burst of laughter from the audience. Guruji continued, "People say life is a struggle or life is a bleep."

James had a smile because he had, in the past, often made statements like this but hearing it from a spiritual person was both funny as well as astute and memorable.

Guruji had a smile too as he proceeded, "People often think mistakenly that you need to conquer the external world or prove your worth, when in reality, the conquest lies within. The struggle is within because you are not aware of yourself within hence you are always confused or reacting to the world rather than being proactive."

The audience had their eyes deadlocked on the Guru and seemed to be moved by his words. He had total command of their attention now.

"Once you win your internal battle and become self-aware, you will have solved most of your physical, physiological and psychological problems."

Suddenly a voice from the audience was heard and a hand waved, seeking permission to speak. It was the same person who had wanted to ask a question in the morning when Guruji was explaining the seven concentric layers of life. This time though, Guruji asked him to stand up and ask the question, but not before he uttered, "I must congratulate you for your patience as you have been waiting to ask me a question since this morning. Looks like your internal battle is waiting to explode. Please ask your question."

The man said, "Thank you, I listened to your lovely insights and thoughts throughout the morning and this afternoon. My question is in connection with your latest pronouncement that all problems can be cured from within. Does that mean we do not need medicines to cure a viral fever or a pill for a bad headache?"

James thought, that is a smart-ass question, 'I am curious to hear Guruji's comeback line'.

"That's an excellent question, I guess all that patience has paid off. Son, what's your name?"

"Shravanan," he replied.

"Shravanan. OK, what do you do?"

"I am a Pharmacist."

"No wonder you asked that question regarding the medicines. After all, you are the ones who give us pills along with the bills!"

Shravanan was smiling though also slightly embarrassed.

Guruji continued, "You have made my job simpler. Tell me, how many surgeries have you performed?"

"Not even one. Why would I perform surgeries? I fill in prescriptions, not perform surgeries!"

James thought that was a smart answer.

Guruji said, "See, that's exactly my point. You have an awareness of what you can do. You know the ins and outs of medicines so you can give out medicines as per the prescriptions and make them aware of the dos and don'ts about their health condition and the medication, but if anyone asks you a question about surgery you would direct them to the competent person in that field. Using the same analogy, you can also proactively implement similar dos and don'ts to prevent your body from many diseases. Your self-awareness will enable you to proactively apply preventive hygiene mechanisms, and avoid many illnesses upfront. See, Awareness is both 'Prevention' and 'Cure'.

"Awareness enables you to be proactive in your decision-making process to stop you from falling into the 'catching up' mode. Further to that, if any such situations present themselves due to certain unforeseen reasons, then it helps you to 'come out' of it by making the right decisions through your Intellect layer. So, if you are aware of your general health but do get a viral fever or a headache, you can handle that health traction more effectively.

"Let me give you another analogy which will resonate with everyone in the audience. All of you earn to make a living, be it through a job, self-employment or by running a business. When you are aware of your overall financial status and annual earnings, it is much easier for you to create spending plans and handle monetary transactions efficiently. However, if you are not aware of your overall financial status, you can neither plan nor react or respond to monetary transactions coming up in front of you."

James was finding all this highly revealing.

"Awareness is not a thing, it is the background to the things happening across our human concentric layers. Awareness exists in every human by birth. The key is to know how to raise our awareness level and strengthen it. It's like a sport where, the more you practice, the better you get at it. "Similarly, the more you strengthen your awareness, the more you start playing in the zone of 'Prevention' rather than in the 'Cure' zone."

'Awareness is like a sport? What the hell does this mean?' James went into his monologue mode. This was another new learning for him beyond any B-School. He quickly returned his attention to the revealing talk.

"Let me put it this way, if you are the hero, awareness is like your sidekick or wingman. It is always with you without making itself so obvious. It makes you rethink all your decisions, gives you clarity and most importantly, makes you take the right decisions, no matter how hard they are. At the end of the day, awareness helps you filter distractions and understand which thoughts demand and deserve your attention.

"Let me share with you another example right here, right now. Just a two-minute walk away from here. No, I am not talking about the pantry but about the library."

Again, Guruji was able to bring a smile to the faces of his audience.

"I guess most of you have gone through the library of the Ashram. Did you notice the various labels marked on the shelves, clearly defining the various genres or types of books? Now imagine if those books were placed randomly around the library, you would end up spending your time searching for the books you want rather than reading them. Plus, you would be directionless and struggling to find the book of your choice. How would you feel if a mythological story is placed next to a biography and then the very next book turns out to be a fantasy?

"Every library should be systematically arranged, be well coordinated and not disorganised. Think if that library was your mind, how chaotic it would be. You would never be aware of the right emotions and feelings at the required time. What's worse? You wouldn't be able to pick up a positive emotion from the shelf of your mind, thus leading to negativity, confusion and anxiety. The importance is to pick up one emotion at a time just like you would pick up one book at a time in a library."

James couldn't agree more as he had plenty of mental demons running unfettered in his own mind.

"The panacea of all your problems lies within. You have to pick, choose and channelize emotions by becoming aware of things inside you and around you. With awareness running in the background across all concentric layers, you become conscious of your thoughts and feelings, one at a time."

James thought that the Guru had been outfoxed but then he was proven wrong yet again. The Guru was a master at making comebacks.

With that, Guruji called it a day, but not before making everyone do a few breathing exercises and chatting with the audience one on one, making sure he made everyone comfortable.

For now, James felt as if he was in a place called dreamland. As he was becoming aware of his thoughts, several questions were looming large in his head - 'Guruji's talk about awareness was insightful but how can it be compared with any sport as he described? Sporting activity is a game where players practice and train everyday but awareness is not a sport nor a game... The A of awareness in *ABCD* is fascinating but how can awareness be strengthened? And what do *BCD* stand for...?'

James was curious and looking forward to the next session on how to raise and strengthen awareness levels. For now, he was looking to raise his athletic levels by taking a jog before the setting of the sun.

CHAPTER 6
The Awareness Workout

Dinner was simple yet succulent. The ambience of the Ashram was enhanced thanks to the full moon night, the fireflies buzzing, crickets chirping and the sound of water streaming down from the river Ganga. It brought plenty of music to any nature lover's ear. All this added to the flavour of the food. James was slurping dal, Indian lentils, while questions were still popping up in his head like thought blurbs in comic books. After dinner, Guru Manvik asked James, "So, how was your dinner?"

James said, "On a lighter note, my taste buds were *aware* of every ingredient that went into making the dishes so delicious. Guruji grinned and said, "Looks like your sense of humour is getting flavourful. Now let's 'get down to business' as you would say in the corporate world."

Suddenly the corporate world flashed in front of James' eyes.

"Are you with me James?" Guru Manvik asked.

"Of course, I am".

"Thinking of your good old corporate days, I guess."

James was shocked, suddenly feeling as if the Guruji was reading his mind. He replied, "I guess your awareness levels about people is mind-blowing. I was completely fascinated by your talk, earlier in the day, about awareness. Is it possible to strengthen or exercise your awareness levels?"

"That's an excellent question James, if I observe you right now, I see a man who likes to pick up weights in the gym and exercise regularly. Right?"

"Right on the money, yet again."

"Tell me James, were you always muscular like this or did you work hard to grow them in the gym?"

"Well, I have realised now that nothing comes easy in life. You have to work out hard, diet and sleep well to gain muscle size, definition and tonality."

"That's exactly my point, James. Just like you increase your muscle mass, you can also increase your awareness levels by exercising certain techniques. These can amplify your awareness levels, taking them to a new high."

"Really, what are they, would you please tell me?"

"Absolutely James, but let's go step by step instead of jumping ahead too soon. Let's pick three scenarios."

He drew a small chart with the following points:

- Senses push vs Sense objects pull
- Outside-in vs Inside-out.
- Most disconnected vs most connected.

James replied, "Sorry, but that seems alien to me. Could you elaborate in plain English?"

"Most certainly I will."

"In the process of raising our awareness levels, these are the simple foundational building blocks – similar to learning alphabets before learning any language.

"Remember I told you earlier about the senses in our body, which are the skin, ears, nose, eyes and tongue? And I also covered sense objects, which are anything that your sense organs pick up. For example, when you hear a beautiful song, the ear gets interested. Similarly, when you bite into a slice of pizza, it is a treat for your taste buds so there is a pull of the sense objects. Let me give you another analogy. Imagine, you are listening to a beautiful track while driving down the highway. It's just another day returning from work. Suddenly, you spot a crowd of people along the road. Your eyes look at the animated crowd and your ears hear the commotion around. These two senses react to the situation, which makes you either slow down or stop your car. Next, you will mute your music and try and hear about the incident from those gathered there. It could be an accident or a mishap along the highway. One thing is for sure, you are not that cold-hearted to just drive away without giving two hoots about the situation."

James looked at Guruji and asked, "So what is the push and pull phenomenon here?" Guruji replied, "It's simple James, your eyes and ears in this case push you while the crowd and the commotion pulled your senses towards them. Hence, it's simple – senses push, sense objects pull."

James replied, "Very insightful. So you are telling me that the next time I enter my place and I smell something really appetizing, my nose pushes me to the source of the smell whereas the food in the kitchen or on the stove become the sense objects, which are pulling me to the food?"

"Now you are becoming aware James. I can also see that you thoroughly enjoyed your dinner so that's a fair analogy. This is a simple yet powerful workout in raising your awareness levels, James. Every time, keep reminding yourself and be aware of the fact that senses push, sense objects pull."

"This brings me to my next point which has a connection to the narrative of my first one - senses and sense objects, and how we perceive them in the external world.

"What come to your mind when I say 'Outside-in v/s Inside-out'? Confused? Don't be. Let me simplify it with a question: what do you see all around us?"

James looked around and said, "Plenty of flora and fauna. I can also hear the sound of the gushing waves of the river Ganga."

"Glad you like it here James. Wonderful observation. Now tell me, can you hear your own heartbeat or see your own internal organs?"

James said, "No, I would need a stethoscope to hear my heartbeat or take a few scans to see my own body."

"Excellent going James, you were scratching your skin a while back, why did you do that?"

"Felt a couple of mosquitos on my skin."

"Ok, so you could feel the slightest touch of the mosquito but nothing when it comes to the fast flowing of blood in your veins?"

Guruji grinned, "Isn't it unique that the most advanced form of design, which we call 'human engineering' has five sense organs which can sense any and everything externally but can't see or notice anything inside your own body?"

James was left with his eyes wide open.

"This is a simple yet another powerful workout in raising your awareness level. So, every time, keep reminding yourself and be aware of the fact: 'outside-in v/s inside-out'.

"This brings to me the next point, "What comes to your mind when I say the word 'connected'?"

James pauses for a moment and says, "Well, I can think

of the internet, social media, broadband, travelling and video chat."

Guruji smiles and says, "Looks like a day in the office for James, but yes, you have hit the right note. We all are living in a world where technology, which seemed science fiction a few years ago, has actually become a reality. Smartphones, the internet, artificial intelligence and robots are just a few of them. And now we are trying to connect interplanetary by colonizing Mars and the Moon. That's the level of technology we are talking about. You can snapchat with your friends on the other side of the planet within seconds and at the tap of a button. It's truly remarkable, isn't it?"

James looks him in the eye and said, "Absolutely!"

Guruji retorted, "Not quite."

James is perplexed, "You are asking a question, answering it and then not agreeing with it. Can't understand."

"That's because the word 'connected' has become a very superficial, technological and physical term. While we all can see that human evolution has been at its fastest in the external world, it has also led to us being disconnected faster and far worse than ever before. These are not mere statements James. I have the stats too. Nearly 300 million people around the world suffer from depression every year. More than 250 million people suffer from anxiety disorders. What does this show us, James?"

James nodding his head says, "It means we are not connected with our thoughts, feelings and emotions."

"Exactly. Even despite all the technological advancements and upgrades, our human engineering has been downgraded over the years. That explains how the wellbeing industry has become an industry netting billions of dollars today. In reality these things come from within and cannot be purchased in the outside world. Peace is not a commodity and nor is love or honesty. These come from what you experience within."

These new facts coming to light were like the twinkling stars in the night sky.

James was just marvelling at the stars, as well as those words from Guruji as he replied, "That's so true!"

CHAPTER 7
Awareness lights the night sky

"Don't be surprised James, human engineering has something even better in store for us."

"What's that?"

"Experiences!"

"Didn't get it."

"James, while our sense organs have been designed to perceive the outer world, the experience of these perceptions take place in your inner world."

James was in awe of Guruji as he said, "Now that is one hell of a statement."

"Which you can turn into heaven for you. This includes all the concentric layers, personas and anatomy of human engineering I had covered earlier today.

"Taking the earlier example of falling in love with the girl next door, I would say, first, the girl appeals to your sense organs. Next, you feel connected to her not only in the external world but also in your internal world as she is the reason for your inner peace, bliss, love and for the confidence in yourself. This makes you experience various emotions, feelings and memories with that girl. Clear, right?"

"Crystal," James replied.

Guruji then asked him a seemingly unrelated question out

of the blue. "What is your weight?"

"Why?"

"Ok fine, if you don't want to tell me, I understand. Anyway, men, these days, are also very figure-conscious, health-conscious and more informed, just like women. At least tell me, the unit for weight."

"kilogram", James replied.

"And for liquid?"

"Litre".

Excellent, "What about Life?"

"Life does not have a unit Guruji".

"Oh, yes it does and it is measured in something I just mentioned – 'Experience'. If you experience happiness, your life turns happy. If you think pessimistically, your experience unit will turn negative. 'Experience' is the most dynamic unit in life."

James had goose bumps as he said, "My God, I always thought I am the wise guy and Mr know-it-all but this revelation makes me feel as though I am but a novice with regard to life. Never thought human engineering had so much depth. It is all starting to make sense now and I still have so much more to learn."

"James, you must be thinking that the outer world affects the experiences of our inner world. Actually it is the other way around, which so many people haven't yet decoded in life. If your fortress has weak defensive walls then every Tom, Dick and Harry will attack and affect your reactions. That's what gives rise to inner conflict and self-doubt. The idea is to make the inner world so strong that no matter what happens on the outside, your kingdom of the inner world is always safe and secure."

James asked, "How do you do that?"

"Remember, you earlier wanted to know the exercises to increase your awareness levels? I was giving you some context to awareness before I got into the exercises. Guess you understand where I am coming from. As I said, you need to learn the alphabets before learning any language. Keep reminding yourself of the three nuggets I shared – the more you become aware of 'senses push, sense objects pull', 'outside-in v/s inside-out', you will start raising your awareness levels to connect with your inner world of experiences, and move away from 'most disconnected' to most 'connected'."

"Oh Guruji, I know where you are coming from and where you are going with this and I love every minute of this journey."

"Leonardo Da Vinci once said, simplicity is the ultimate sophistication so let me make this really simple. James, believe it or not, the exercise I am about to reveal is no rocket science, it is as simple as raising your finger. I call it the *finger-wonder game*'. I know in the corporate world everyone is good at pointing fingers at others, but here, you will be pointing the finger towards yourself. So, here's how it goes."

The next thing Guruji asked James was to raise his hand in front of his eyes. Right in the centre of the two eyeballs, just above his nose. Next, he told him to raise his index finger.

Guruji was focused on James as he said, "What do you see in front of you?"

"I see my index finger right in the middle."

"That's great James, now focus on it for the next 30 seconds."

James was focusing on his finger like a hunter on its prey. He was dead-still and did not move his eyeballs for even a second. He held his poise and composure as nothing bothered him. Till a few days ago he was one of the most dysphoric persons in the world and also the most wanted man in the US media and law circles. Guruji noticed his remarkable progress. Interrupting his concentration he queried, "Ok James, tell me what you saw in the last 30 seconds."

"I just saw my finger and nothing else."

"Are you sure? Describe the background to me."

"I can't, it was a complete blur."

"Fantastic to know that. Now I want you to do the reverse. Do everything as you did before but this time, focus on the background, not on your finger."

James did as he was told. Now he was focusing on the background like a cameraman for the picture-perfect shot.

After 30 seconds, Guruji asked him, "So what did you see James?"

"Guruji, my finger was invisible as I could only see the background. Nothing else"

"Excellent James, so what have you learned from this exercise?"

"Improving my focus, I guess."

"It's more than that James, this exercise is a splendid example of awareness. When you were focused on the index finger, you were conscious of your awareness levels and things in the foreground. Everything else was in blur mode. Much like the portrait mode on your smartphone, isn't it? When you concentrated on the background, you lost sight of your internal world and awareness. That's how the finger became invisible to you."

James was absolutely speechless. He couldn't believe that something so simple could actually be so profound. 'Indeed, simplicity is the ultimate sophistication', he murmured to himself.

"Always do this exercise, when you are losing sight of things or if stress is clouding your mind. It will put things back in perspective. Remember the library example I quoted earlier? It is up to you to decide which emotion or feeling you want to play in the foreground and lose sight of other tasks, emotions and negativity."

James realized that this is what made Guru Manvik way different from any other he had imagined or come across. Guruji crafted two real-life and modern examples without getting too dogmatic about religion, spirituality and the silly remedies a lot of people fall for.

"The next exercise I am about to give you, James, will not only raise your awareness levels but transform them forever. However, do not expect any overnight miracles. You will have to attain awareness with diligence and hard work. Just like the gym and diet examples I gave you earlier. Initially, you will have to work hard for awareness but then, over a period of time, awareness will start working for you."

James had only heard about the thing in corporate circles that said 'don't work for money but let the money work for you'. Though, this adage was far from reality in the big corporate empires. He asked, "is this exercise tougher than the *finger-wonder?*"

"No, it is not, it's quite simple, all you have to do is at night when you retire for the day and first thing in the morning after you wake up. This exercise is called *Introspection & Imagination (I&I)*. Please remember the two *I*'s in *I&I* are distinct and different. Let's take them one by one. When I say 'Introspection', all you have to do is to remember the various activities of your whole day. Whether it was bad at work or with the boss or for that matter a date with your partner at the end of the evening. The key here is to see the day like a movie playing in your head without being judgemental or biased. Don't point at follies or goodness. Just pay heed to the details right from the time you got out of bed. All you have to do is to be aware minus analysing any moment. Don't ask *'why is it happening'* just focus on *'what is happening'.*"

"That is easier said than done," James retorted.

"I agree. That is why I told you it is not going to be an overnight wonder. That is where the role of the second *I, Imagination,* comes in. So, hear me out. Let's assume that you are introspecting a day that was not so great. Once you are done, imagine if the same situation arose the next day, how would you tackle it? Would you try something different? Will you use some other technique, tool or approach, which could change the situation or the people in your favour? Again, don't analyse, just imagine. Stop the ifs and buts."

"How will this help me?" James enquired, a tad impatiently.

"Slow and steady my friend. This activity will ensure that your mind and emotions are in sync with your awareness levels. Through this exercise, you sharpen your awareness skills like a craftsman uses a chisel to carve out a beautiful statue. It takes time, effort and skill. But then, no masterpieces were made in a day. Not even our planet earth."

"What we see today around us is the evolution of millions of years of the chemical, physical and biological changes our earth has undergone. It is a masterpiece for us to survive and thrive in today but it wasn't always like this. The greatest advantage of this exercise is that it will help you pick and choose decisions and emotions in crunch situations, which all of us face in life these days."

Guruji has his razor-sharp eye on James now. " It's time to take your awareness places before you sleep. Tell me, James, what do you normally do before sleeping?"

James replied, "Normally I would watch some TV, surf my social media pages and reply to a few emails or chats."

Guruji had a smile on his face, "That explains half of your problems and insinuations."

James had a clueless look on his face.

"James, what if I asked you to visualize something right now, what would that be?"

"I see an ocean right now in front of me with a few kingfishers sitting on a tree. I am holding a fishing rod in one hand and a glass of wine in the other. There's a beautiful woman, clad in a swimsuit, chilling beside my little, luxurious, wooden cottage. I have my own private boat on which I cruise and party with my friends. All in all, I can visualize my own private island."

"James, I must say, you have quite a vivid sense of imagination. Awareness is a lot about introspection and imagination."

"What else do you have in store for me Guruji?"

"Plenty, but these life lessons are not fast food James. You have to enjoy the *ABCD* of life like a four-course meal in proper intervals. Too much food or eating too soon is bad for digestion. Why don't you just absorb and become aware of things for the next two days? Let's meet at sunrise after that. Dawn is the best time when the first light of day makes its way to earth. The light in the foreground complements the enlightening of the mind in the background. So, before we start learning about breathing, I would suggest: just breathe easy."

James is back to his monologue mode. 'Perhaps, Guruji is right, I do need to give myself some time and space.' As he inhaled the salubrious air and took the last sip of his green tea, his cup was now empty but his mind was full of the refreshing thoughts that had been planted there by Guruji.

Learning about the *A* of *ABCD* and the *'finger wonder game'* and *'Introspection & Imagination'* techniques were a revelation to him. His hugest takeaway was learning to focus on *'what'* instead of *'why'*.

Returning to his room, James began taking his awareness to some of the events of his past. With his eyes closed, he endeavoured to see them with the sight of *'what'* instead of *'why'*. It was easier said than done as he kept getting distracted every second. The next thing he knew was that everything turned pitch black as he dozed off. But when he opened his eyes, he couldn't believe what he saw next.

He was rejoicing in *ABCD* and becoming curious to learn more of it as he dozed off again…

CHAPTER 8
You will regret this one day

The voice of a man came ringing or rather stinging to his ears.

James had gone into his 'bulls and bears' days which were the complete opposite of the serene, calm and meditative state afforded by the Ashram. Back then, James was in the financial markets, which could make one a hero or zero within a few microseconds. Investment banking and financial markets are thankless. You had to be on your toes every nanosecond.

"You will regret this", the voice of a man came ringing, rather stinging to his ears.

As he walked into his office every morning, there was an aura that surrounded him and followed him like his shadow. It was made up of ambition, aspiration and aggression. He was a role model for some and a fall guy for others. As he made his way to the 22nd floor, there was a catch-22 situation. The financial data that had been fed into the system was delayed and erroneous. That resulted in a major standoff between James and the Risk Head, Amit Vyas. What was even worse, the markets were supposed to open in a matter of minutes.

Just then, James was interrupted by the secretary of the Managing Director who announced, "The boss wants to see you."

"Great, I knew that was coming. In fact, I want to see him too. Can't work with such shit going around," James muttered to himself as he glanced over at the Risk Head, Amit.

"Watch your words" said Amit.

"And you watch the numbers and data before giving your suggestions," James countered.

He stormed off the scene before another storm could come his way.

"Hi Mathew! Good to see you, how's it going?"

"I am fine." Mathew Prior was a man of integrity, guts and composure. Three traits that were priceless in the financial strata. He had recently replaced Houton Waugh who was fired for being a mole in the system and indulging in insider trading. Prior was a natural choice as he had an impeccable record.

"The market is opening in about 20 minutes James, just wanted to discuss something with you."

"If you want to talk about this morning's incident, how can we work with a Risk Head like that?"

"James, right now you should be focusing not on petty fights but the Netflix shares. In the next 2-3 days, I expect a winter breeze".

"Oh, I thought you are talking about a storm that's coming."

"Well there was a storm in the office with you losing your temper. We will talk about the morning incident sometime later during lunch."

"Sorry, I will be eating some big stocks during that time,

see ya later" James intoned, more to himself. James left without even looking back. Frankly, he was done for the day even before it had started. When Mathew spoke about the storm and winter breeze, they were not discussing the weather, it was an analogy of the stock market. Usually the phrase, 'a storm is coming' means a heavy sell-out while 'a winter breeze' denotes rumours of selling with the markets usually ending up green.

If one thought that the office was a stormy place then the trading floor was a tsunami of data, investors, numbers and algorithms, flowing in every which direction per microsecond. There was a war cry every second to buy or sell a particular stock. No, there were no breathers here. Just marching orders if you don't get the job done right. The whole uncertainty was something that seduced James. He thrived in this challenging atmosphere. After all, it was all about the money honey. Yes, all markets do have regulatory authorities and watchdogs but nobody plays it by the book here. That's natural, considering there was more money and less time. Insider trading was standard practice, which even the outsiders knew.

The war-like situation on the trading floor generated another encounter between the Risk Head, Amit, and James.

James said, "Thanks for a wonderful morning. Amit, are you even serious about working here? You still use old systems, tools and techniques. Wake up man! When are you going to upgrade your systems? We are in the 21st century, not in the stone age. This is unacceptable."

Amit looked angrily at him and replied, "Alright, Mr. wise guy, if you think you have a system or tools, why don't you just build it. After all, you are known to the world as the 'go-getter' or 'Mr. Millennial' who is to be featured in Time

Magazine. But in this office we all know how brash, snooty and egotistical you are. I guess my next meeting will be with you and Matt, in his office, as talking to you is like talking to a wall."

"Well, at least I offer support as a wall! At least I am not some fuddy-duddy who can't think ahead standing in one of the top investment banking firms in the world. I have just two words for you, 'fuck off'."

Amit's face was blood-red with anger as he replied, **"You will regret this one day."**

James woke up with a start. He had been dreaming. He was afraid, and did regret being a hard ass and a wannabe. He thought he could break the rules of the game being a new kid on the block. He had not paid heed to what his mentor had always told him, 'it is important to know the rules before you break them'.

Here he was sitting on his bed in an Ashram having left everything behind. His mind had gone deep down into his consciousness to search for incidents that were affecting him. If he thought that this was the only one, he was mistaken. There came another statement buzzing in his ears as he dozed off again.

"You are not aware of what you just said to me."

This time it was a woman's voice seething in his ears as he went into nostalgia. It was Eliza, his ex-girlfriend. He was reliving the past right in front of his eyes.

An episode of a showdown with Eliza appears before him. James had met Eliza at a fashion show in Milan. What started out as an exchange of numbers on the fashion runway, quickly turned into spending quality time at discreet getaways. They were inseparable. She quickly became his partner, confidant and counsellor. She was the sanest part of his insane corporate life.

That's why he had confided in her, which led to plenty of high voltage passion as well as pain between the two of them.

An average human brain has the ability to store 2.5 million gigabytes of digital memory. It's strange how the human brain synapses can link two identical situations and responses buried deep within for years. James's brain was connecting the episode of Amit with Eliza. After all, it was that particular episode where Eliza started questioning his state of affairs and maintaining decorum in the office.

"James, I was right there listening to your verbal tiff with Amit, you must apologize to him at once."

"Are you crazy? Some people deserve it."

"Says who?"

"Says the best man on the floor for the last continuous four years. And that's a fact. Even after working with jokers like Amit, I am able to earn the dollars for this company."

"What about earning respect James, when are you going to learn that?"

"If you are so great then why is Matt sitting in that corner office instead of you? Maybe, he's the old war horse here or that he's got more grey hair than me. By the way that day is not far off."

"Mr James Hatman, you are never wrong." Eliza said in a sharp and sarcastic tone which made James extremely defensive.

"Maybe I am wrong in sharing everything with you. After all, you are always judging me. Come with solutions and not problems. Whose side are you on?"

"I am on the side of right. Don't expect me to sit back and be one of those people who say yes boss, ok boss or whatever boss. Such people add no value neither do they let you grow personally or professionally. James, let's agree to disagree. It will help us both to plug areas in life which make us vulnerable. If you needed a yes-person then why have a partner? A payslip worker would do, right? And these so-called people who always make you happy treat you just like you trade a stock. Today, you are like a brand or commodity which is making money. People are ready to put a bet on you but what happens when you fail one fine day? It will be interesting to see if even one of them will stand by your side on that day."

James looked frustrated now, "Look Eliza, this is becoming a daily affair now. I think I made a big mistake in mixing my professional life with my personal life. I have a million things running in my mind and then I have to put up with your daily rants and squabbles."

"James, you are worth a million things to me and I do not want you to fall into the wrong hands or situations."

"You are talking to one of the most successful investment bankers today so stop being my granny and telling me what to do and what not to do. I am not some kid. I have seen life more than you. Today, people call you James Hatman's girlfriend."

Totally pissed off with James, Eliza yelled," Fuck you, James. How dare you talk to me like that? Have you forgotten the basic ethics of talking to a woman? You are one of the most narcissistic, pompous, cocky and materialist people I have ever come across. You know what, I am leaving. Can't remain here for even another minute."

James got sarcastic, "How about 30 seconds? Eliza come on, you are taking this too far, I am sorry, didn't mean what I said but you really are not helping me by questioning my ambitions, aspirations and motives every day."

Eliza had a tear running down her cheek as she said, "You are a bad liar and not very good at apologising.

"James, you are not aware of what you just said to me."

The next second he saw Eliza charging out of the office and shutting the door on him.

James again woke up – he was sweating and shaking. His eyes were wide open in panic and felt as if countless pins and needles were pricking him. He gulped down two glasses of water and slowly came back to his senses. He then recalled Guruji's session on *'Introspection and Imagination'* and decided to relive the same incidents, this time while awake. He started becoming aware of both episodes, but this time, with a different approach - he was focusing on *'What is happening'* instead of *'Why is it happening'*. He noticed something profoundly different for the first time in his life. As he was visualizing both episodes from the perspective of *'what'*, rather than *'why'*, he felt as if he was 'witnessing' a movie clip in front of his eyes, rather than someone engulfed in it as a 'victim'.

His mind was calm and composed. This time he opened his eyes with a gentle smile as the clip got over. He became aware of the power of the Introspecting exercise of *'what'* instead of *'why'*. He also used the 'Imagination' exercise to ponder upon what he would do differently should a similar situation arise.

For him, it was a whole new world of experience. Though *ABCD* and the seven concentric layers of human engineering were making complete sense....he was also thinking, is this really my cup of tea?

CHAPTER 9

Once upon a time over a cup of tea

James was stirring his tea with a spoon after putting a little sugar in it. As he took the first sip in the Ashram canteen, he looked across the table at the man sitting in front of him. Guruji had a bright smile while his eyes were fixated on James as though he was studying his every move.

James felt overwhelmed and said, "Guruji your session about awareness was simply amazing."

His mellow voice was music to James' ears as he began speaking, "That's nice to hear but why do I sense anxiety in your voice? I couldn't help but notice your troubled state of mind. Something is bothering you. A few minutes ago, I saw your eyes open and close with panic as though someone had pricked you with plenty of pins and needles. Each prick felt as if it came from someone very close to you who had warned you of something to which you paid no heed.

"Earlier, you were extremely wary of me being another so-called Guru on the planet who fleeces people and makes a mockery of their emotions."

James nearly dropped the cup of tea he was holding. He was absolutely shocked and began thinking in his mind, 'how could he read my mind? Did someone tell him about my past'?

"Wondering how I guessed or knew so many things?" Guruji enquired.

"Yes Guruji, I am....and also, a thought has been looming in my mind since this morning – 'is *ABCD* really my cup of tea'?"

"James, I was once the man you were - wild, free, belligerent, intelligent and egotistical."

So, after James had had enough visions and versions of his bad dreams and flashbacks, it was time for Guruji to talk about his.

Guruji began talking about his version of events, "James I know the first question that struck you was me being a Cambridge and MIT (Massachusetts Institute of Technology) student and yet I am here teaching something that goes against the whole scientific community. You see, therein lies a problem. These select few so-called intellectuals think that they own science. Years ago, I was one of them. I thought the subject 'spiritual science' was bogus and I used to laugh at students who were learning it. I felt the western world was all about scientific reasoning, logical experiments and proven theories that could not be questioned. My left brain was in full swing as I completed my course and was fascinated with robots back then.

"The next thing I knew, I was part of the robotics engineering solutions. We know how Artificial Intelligence, Internet of Things and Robotics have an enormous role to play in the future. Somehow, I saw this transformation happening a few decades ago. I was working my butt off night and day. I created a few robot prototypes back then, a project, which was funded by the US government. They were mighty impressed with me and gave me a freehand to pick and choose a team to build an entire line of robots. Everyone started calling me Roboman. I became the most popular kid on the block. I literally became so obsessed with my work and academics that everything else took a backseat. Success got to my young brain as I hired and fired people at will."

James felt as though Guruji was talking about him. He realised that they both had so much in common. He kept listening intently to every word as Guruji continued to speak.

"I was putting in 16 to 20 hours every day, which included plenty of rock and roll. It was not just my profession but my life had also become robotic and mechanical. In a few years, I had everything. A fancy house, car, women and a top corporate and academic position. Then one day, it all came crashing down when I was at the peak of my career. James, always remember, you might climb the ladder of success but when things go wrong, you will have no ladder to come down with. It will be freefall right from the top, knocking you down, perhaps for ever.

"It was my health that went from bad to worse. I went to several top specialists, ate a huge laundry list of medications, pills and portions. I underwent several diagnostic tests and was in pain from the minute I got up till the time I crashed on my bed. Worse, doctors had no definitive answers, all my tests were normal and the medications offered only cosmetic relief. Even with an expansive knowledge in science and physics I had no answer to my problems. It was as if a little bit of me was dying every day.

"From being a showstopper, I became a recluse. I got depressed, drank heavily, felt pain, had medication and this vicious cycle kept repeating itself. Guess what happened one day?"

James had a clueless look on his face with no answer to Guruji's question.

"I overdosed on some anti-depressants to get rid of all my pain, once and for all, and I nearly died. Thanks to a friend of mine who rushed me to the hospital, I survived. He saved my life and that's why I am here, talking to you. That day I realized, perhaps death had another appointment with me. It was going to choose a time and place of its liking, not mine. I had to make the most of my second life. I couldn't find death in the hospital but I definitely found life, which came my way in the form of a piece of paper."

James was in awe of what Guru Manvik was telling him. He was curious to know what was coming next.

"While flipping the pages of a newspaper I read this advert about an Indian Guru, Shiv Hari, who was in America to talk about 'spiritual healing'. I didn't read or rather didn't take in the first word seriously. My eyes were focused on the word 'healing'. I was so desperate, searching for an elixir to cure my pain. So, I decided to go to this event. Do you know what's funny James?"

James was once again clueless.

Guruji continued, "James when I first saw you enter, your body language was exactly the same as mine was, years ago. That's why I could connect to your emotions the minute you stepped in. I even told Parth that you remind me of my younger or darker version. You know, initially, I couldn't care less what Guru Shiv Hari was saying but suddenly the Guru made me stand up and talk about myself. So, I gave a brief intro about myself and my professional life. He told me he was mighty impressed with me but then there was this one thing he said that produced my eureka moment."

James now had his eyes and ears focused on him as he said, "And what was that, Guruji?"

Guruji looked intently at James as he said, "He told me that he could see that my hardware was in great shape but my software seemed corrupted. He then added that no robot can function without proper inputs, programming language or software. I wondered how he knew about me when I was actually meeting him that day for the first time. I was not even on the internet or social media. In fact, at that time the internet was in its nascent stage and social media was non-existent. When I asked him the same question later, he said: 'consider me as your anti-virus software, which can detect, protect and eject the negative software coming into your hardware'. My only question was: what is this software that he is talking about?

Guru Shiv Hari said, "It's your thoughts and emotions. They have the power to heal your body."

James couldn't believe that he had the same question. He felt after all, there was some deep connection between the two of them.

Guruji said with a wry smile, "At first, I thought this made no sense, and is it really my cup of tea? But the more deeply I thought about it, the more my inner voice said that it does make sense. Our thoughts and emotions have the power to hurt us. I guess, I had too many issues lying unaddressed for far too long. It was time to unpack all those thoughts, emotions and feelings. And for that I had to pack my bags and head to a place where I hadn't been before – India."

James could feel the tangible sense of calm that exuded from Guruji when he uttered the word 'India'.

"From being in the driver's seat for years, I suddenly had

to take a backseat in my own life. That's when I decided to quit my job, take a sabbatical and traverse the roads less taken.

After coming to India, I decided to spend time with Guru Shiv Hari. It was he who enlightened me on the subject of human engineering. "During the course of my stay I realized how my hard disk – my human mind - was damaged. Buried deep me were so many feelings and emotions which had not come out. Right from treating people badly at work and even in my personal life, I was a total wreck. Through human engineering Guru Shiv Hari taught me the secrets of curbing and releasing those emotions and expanding my rational side to handle those feelings. That's where I learnt the art and science of human engineering which was the toughest degree in the world to earn, but James once you do, believe me, you can handle any complex problem or pressure-cooker situation in the world with simplicity and maturity."

James asked, "What happened next in your journey?"

Guru Manvik closed his eyes and took a deep breath, "James what happens when a soldier takes bullets in the battlefield?"

James replied in an instant, "He needs hospitalization and surgery to remove all the bullets in order for him to survive and recuperate."

"Well said. I had plenty of bullets in various layers of my human engineering. Some were physical, while others were mostly emotional and mental, which had damaged me from inside. My Guru removed them one by one through his philosophy of the *ABCD* of living."

"*ABCD?*" enquired James.

"Yes James."

Now Guru Manvik looked straight into James and

said, "That's life James. As simple as that. Yet we all love to complicate it."

James looked at him and thought, 'Indeed, life is simple, why do we complicate it'?

Guruji went on, "Guru Shiv Hari performed the surgery using these principles and activated various areas of my brain and body which I didn't even know existed. Once activated, my body required the right lubricants and additives to increase my efficiency, learning and productivity. Thanks to a month-long regimen of a dedicated detox diet and yoga, I began to see changes. It took almost a year but the results were amazing. I was a transformed person, mind, body and soul."

"So, when do I get to learn the rest of this remarkable *ABCD*?"

"Let's not jump the gun, James. First get the A right."

James listened intently. "So, did you go back to work in America or teach here in India?"

"James, you started this conversation over a cup of tea. Remember you need to simmer the tea at the right temperature, add the flavours and find the right time to enjoy its taste, richness and nutrition. Similarly, I shall answer that question when the time is right."

The sun was now setting but a number of questions were raising their heads, by the second, in the mind of James. After listening to Guruji's journey he was convinced that this was the right path for him and that he no longer had any reason to raise the question: 'is *ABCD* my cup of tea'?

Tonight, for the first time he understood the difference between the bookish meaning of the word 'awareness' and its pragmatic definition. Practice makes a man perfect; his father had told him often. But sadly, he had never practiced working on his relationships. Tonight, he wanted to practice the *Finger Wonder* and *Introspection and Imagination exercises.* As his awareness levels grew, he noticed a change in his breathing pattern. 'My God, what are these new sensations I am feeling?" The mystery was about to unravel the next morning with just a few breaths. It was time to unlock the mystery of *B – Breathing* as James took a deep breath.

A few years ago...

A man wearing an Armani suit was sitting with his eyes closed in the middle of Central Park, in New York. He seemed unmoved by what was happening around him.

It looked like a monk had undergone a corporate makeover as he sat in the middle of the Park.

This man had just been elevated to the position of CEO of his enterprise. He was sitting on the hot-seat that required him to turn the fortunes of his organisation. But it was not just the bottom line from the audit report he was worried about. He was truly concerned about the lines from an HR report which revealed that the emotional and mental morale of the employees was at an all-time low.

For RK, the brief was clear, to bring the emotional assets of the workforce in sync with the financial assets and performance. For him, it was like a song with its beats not being in tune. He was set to change the game plan in corporate America. To set a new mood of getting things done.

Sitting in the centre of the Park, he did not realise that he had become the centre of attention too. Some people were mocking him while others were gossiping about the events in his life.

RK was unperturbed, he was only aware of the teeming flora and fauna of the park. For him, his vision for the company was crystal clear. He opened his eyes and inhaled deeply...

CHAPTER 10
Emotions take my breath away

B is for Breathing

James exhaled loudly the next morning, thanks to the breath-taking ambience. It was a beautiful morning - the aura of the aurora next to the river Ganga was an ethereal experience. The rippling sound of the river, the gentle whispering breeze in his ears and the fusion of the spiritual hymns at dawn was the best piece of a natural orchestra that James had ever heard in his life. He took a long deep breath to suck in the positive vibes and energy of the place.

Suddenly, James felt a hand on his shoulder but before he could open his eyes a voice commanded him, "Don't open your eyes, let nothing come between you and awareness. Not even me". James recognized the voice. It was Guruji. His hand on James' shoulder added an extra shot of energy to his focus and awareness. It was like a bullet which was fired at James. The only difference, this bullet healed him with peace and positivity. Just with a mere touch, James felt a moment of spiritual exuberance like never before.

"James, we can touch peoples' lives with a mere touch."

James eyes were closed like he was under a spell as he said, "I couldn't agree more Guruji."

"You can get there James, once you have mastered the

ABCD. Let's learn one step at a time or rather one breath at a time, right?"

Guruji had a smile on his face. James slowly opened his eyes. He had tried his hands at weed and other party drugs in the past but his present trance mode was ten times more powerful. Nothing could match this enigmatic rapture.

"Better than your smoking sessions, James?"

James puffed out his chest, shocked at what Guruji just said.

"You are a dangerous man to sit next to."

"That's why very few politicians visit me, not that I miss them."

"Does not surprise me for a second."

"So, what did you feel James when you were breathing the pristine air of the Ashram?"

"Transformative would be the right word."

"Trance feels more apt. Now tell me, what does 'breathing' mean to you?"

"Well, it's like all the other key things in life, food, water and shelter. It is very important."

Guruji smiled. "James, I assume you are a superhero or a superman."

James thought there was a hint of sarcasm in his voice.

"Well, James if you can put all the three on the same pedestal that means you can stay without all of them for a few days, right? Without food and water your body can survive for a few days, but without air? It cannot survive even for a few minutes. Sadly, most people take air for granted, which explains the state of our planet and the increasing, alarming change in the climate. Everybody wants everything free but nobody wants to respect it." James detected a slight vexation in Guruji's voice.

He continued, "Let me ask you something, what do you feel when there is no network on your phone?"

"I feel angry, anxious and frustrated as I cannot connect with people or the happenings on the planet."

"Yes, you would because it has become your extended or external organ these days. It seems Wi-Fi and network signals are more important than air. That's how connected we are to technology and disconnected from our very roots. Just like the network is the vital component for a smartphone, breathing is the most important component for human survival."

James thought about his addiction to the smartphone back in corporate America. Here at the Ashram he did not miss it at all. Here it felt like a liability.

"I am not against technology, just scared about our over-dependence on it". Guruji clarified. "Coming back to the point, in human engineering, breathing is at the heart of the emotional layer of the seven concentric layers we have already covered."

Both of them walked to an area in the Ashram called 'Nirvana'. The name was a perfect fit as it was overlooking the scenic evergreen mountains of the Himalayan ranges. In the foreground, the river Ganga was flowing with smooth curves that would make any sculptor or architect proud. What was even better, the sun was out and its reflection was glistening straight into the Ashram. Guruji requested James to sit cross-legged as he continued talking to him.

"Quite fittingly, we are sitting in Nirvana. No better time to start talking about breathing than daybreak, James. Like awareness activates your intellectual engine and helps you to reason, breathing activates the emotional engine in the human engineering system. Remember, the flight example I had given? Have you ever sat in a flight with one wing?"

"Of course not."

"Exactly! To have the right balance, you need awareness and breathing to work in sync to create the perfect balance of your mind and body. Now James, remember that beautiful scene you described to me last evening, that of your private island?"

"Yes, how can I forget that?"

"Good, so become aware of it once again with your eyes closed, maybe you can add a little more romance to the whole setting."

This time James saw his exotic private island but it seemed jaded in front of the most beautiful woman standing right in front of him. It was Eliza, his ex-girlfriend. She was so near yet so far from him.

"She is beautiful, isn't she James?" Guruji enquired.

The mentalist was predicting and he was right yet again.

James saw Eliza swimming right next to him one minute and lying beside him near a bonfire the very next minute. A train of thoughts was now over speeding in his mind. He thought, 'we were always so happy'.

"How is she looking, James?"

"Just wow."

"And how is your breathing?"

"Slow and relaxed, like I am in a state of Nirvana, literally."

"Yes James, you are right as we speak."

"Ok, now become aware of something which you regret or find extremely disturbing."

James' mind went into rewind mode to that fateful day of his accident which had changed his life forever.

James relived that car crash in his head, watching as the car somersaulted a couple of times like some dinky-car of kids in their backyard. Then he went into blackout mode.

"James, I can see you are in extreme pain, what's your breathing like?"

James was gasping for air and was extremely queasy about what had just flashed in front of him. Guruji asked him to stop and open his eyes. "James not only did your mind-set change with the two scenarios but so did your breathing pattern. Happy emotions invoked long peaceful breaths and troubled memories sparked shorter, choking breaths."

"So, what does that mean? Are you implying that there is a connection between breathing and emotions?"

A few years ago....

From the outside, RK looked as calm as the sunny blue sky. From the inside, there was a tsunami of emotions running through his mind. Nobody looking at him could say that he had just lost his father, and that he was losing his brother to cancer.

Despite all these setbacks, he seemed as resolute as a monk praying in the temples of the Himalayas. That's because he had mastered the art of linking his emotions to his breathing. That's what brought order to his life and to the emotional ecosystem around him.

CHAPTER 11
Breathing: fight or flight
v/s rest and digest

"Absolutely! If we reverse the order, longer breaths have a direct link to happy emotions and shorter breaths with stress and anxiety."

James was under stress most of the time back home, and some of his friends and peers told him to breathe nice and slow in times of crisis when he was exceptionally stressed out. Another advice to which he had paid absolutely no heed. Yet, it made so much sense today when Guruji made him do this little exercise.

"This looks good in theory but what happens when external situations change? I can reverse, but not the world, can I?" James asked with genuine curiosity.

"That's an excellent observation but the answer lies in your very question."

"I don't get you."

"James, when you are reactive to situations, your breathing pattern changes according to the circumstances in the external world. Reversing the situation means you are self-content within and are immune to the happenings around you. This is the inside-out example had told you about."

James looked slightly perplexed as he said, "I thought breathing was just about inhaling and exhaling."

"James, it's a pity that this is what you and millions of people the world over think. It's a shame that we have reduced something as important as breathing to just inhaling and exhaling. Breathing is the most important fuel for your body, important not just to survive but also to thrive."

"How?"

"There are two ways to solve this mystery. The modern scientific understanding and the ancient technique. Which one do you want to go for, first?"

"You decide Guruji."

"Looking at you, I think it best to tackle the modern scientific way first. I am sure you do know that there are two kinds of functions in our nervous system - Involuntary and voluntary functions."

"Not in great detail, but, Ok, so?"

"Involuntary functions are like your heartbeat or digestive processes, which do not ask your permission to perform. It is just like the thoughts running in your head right now wondering why Guruji is talking like my school's biology teacher."

"Yes, that pretty much sums it up." Both of them chuckled in sync.

"On the other hand, voluntary functions are solely at your discretion, which means you are putting in an effort to walk, talk or listen to me by will or by force."

James had a smile on his face. "You never give up a chance to pull my leg!"

"Truth is bittersweet my friend. More bitter than sweet, actually."

"Where does breathing come in, in all this?" James enquired with a tinge of impatience.

"In everything."

"Everything?"

"Breathing cuts across both voluntary and involuntary functions of your body. Breathing is the only voluntary function in the entire body, which has the power to alter your involuntary functions. Tell me James, what will happen if you stopped breathing even for the next one minute?"

"My heart rate will drop. My lungs will feel they are bursting, my blood circulation will slow down and my muscles will cramp up."

"There you go, James. Most of the things you told me are your involuntary functions. Now do you understand how breathing can affect all your involuntary functions? It is similar to the situation where you have any phone - be it an iPhone, a Samsung phone or any other phone –but without a network signal, it has no meaning or purpose."

The example made complete sense to James. He thought, 'this couldn't have been put more aptly'.

"I don't want to sound like your school biology teacher so let me make this short and sweet".

- Voluntary, termed as Somatic nervous system
- Involuntary, termed as Autonomic nervous system
    - o   fight or flight mode, termed as Sympathetic
    - o   rest and digest mode, termed as Parasympathetic

He drew a simple image:

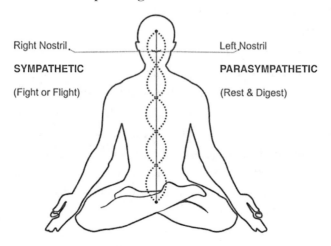

Right Nostril

SYMPATHETIC

(Fight or Flight)

Left Nostril

PARASYMPATHETIC

(Rest & Digest)

Guruji now looked back at James with his eyes fixated on him as though he was ready for another hypnotic spell. He continued: "As I had mentioned earlier about the voluntary functions, it is your Somatic nervous system which comes into play when you volunteer to do something i.e. walking, jogging etc. This is linked more to physical activities. Do you have any doubts?"

"Guruji, so, voluntary function is about making a choice?"

"I am afraid James you have touched upon a topic that needs some considerable understanding. There is a difference between a voluntary function and the choices we make in life. I will come to choices later but just to give you a one-line distinction. Voluntary functions mostly involve the physical or anatomical layer of your body whereas the word 'choice' has a far deeper meaning, much beyond the realms of the physical body into further layers of human engineering and implications in life. I will be touching upon it at the right time and place, James. Life is all about timing, be it a smash on the tennis court or making a decision in the boardroom."

"Couldn't agree more…"

"James for now your mantra should be - breathing is the only voluntary function which has the power to alter your Involuntary functions i.e. Autonomic nervous system."

James' eyes were again fixed on the chart which described the Autonomic nervous system.

Guruji was all smiles again. "Now I am going to delve elaborately into the Involuntary, Autonomic nervous system, which is made up of two parts, *flight or fight,* Sympathetic nervous system and *rest and digest,* Parasympathetic nervous system."

"Here's a question for you, what was early man up against?"

"Many things. Nature, shelter, food, protection and procreation."

"Exactly, well said. The early humans on the planet didn't have a proper place to live or sleep, and there was lack of access to food, clothes and shelter."

"That's right Guruji. Man was moving around like a nomad discovering new creatures, climates and terrains to settle in. He had a constant fear of the unknown. It can be from a tiger someday or being struck down by lightning the next day."

"Spot on James, this has got your adrenaline pumping. In such circumstances, man had two options or choices. Either to fight the situation or to run away as fast as he could, i.e. fly away from the situation. Now tell me, today do we have tigers chasing us down the street or does the weather scare us like it did back then?"

"No, not unless you are homeless, and coming to tigers,

there are very few left anyway."

"Yes, thanks to an advanced species called man." Guruji gasped as he completed the sentence.

"I can read your mind this time, the falling numbers of the environment worry you."

Guruji smiled and quipped, "Looks like the mind-reading illness is becoming infectious."

"Speaking of illness James, remember, I had earlier shared with you some statistics about the steep rise in mental illnesses. Answer this, if people have access to food, water, shelter and technology better than ever before, why is there so much anxiety, stress and strain in society? Why are more and more people suffering with lifestyle related diseases like obesity, anxiety, depression, blood pressure, diabetes and cardiovascular problems? In the earlier days, humans had the fear of wild animals, the fact of no easy access to food and shelter but these days what are we running away from?"

James came back with a quirky remark, "I don't know what we are running away from but we are running after money, money, and more money."

"Yes, you are close. The modern-day version of tigers and lions chasing us are the enormous desires, debts and *habit-to-compare* lifestyles we lead today."

"We are continuously running to compete in the rat race of the so-called 'settled' phenomenon. For some, settled means buying a small flat. For some others buying a mansion is their version of not being settled. Forget that, the youngsters of today are getting depressed about the number of *likes* and followers on their Instagram or Facebook page, thanks to peer pressure and the social media phenomenon. The word *like* has lost its emotional touch today and people are buying *likes* on these channels. It's just another commodity. We are constantly running after *'what-we-don't-have'*, which has put our fight or flight mode into a constant adrenaline overdrive. The modern day *comparing life-style* is becoming key to switching-on to *fight or flight* mode, resulting in commonly prevalent diseases like obesity, depression, anxiety, blood pressure, diabetes and cardiovascular problems. Is this what human evolution was meant for?"

"Definitely not. So, what is the solution?"

"Activating the parasympathetic, *rest & digest mode*. This is the other side of your autonomic nervous system. Just like night has day, winter has summer, *rest & digest* is your stress buster mode. Ever been to a spa James?"

"Absolutely, can't imagine living in the 'lots-to-do' world without a spa treatment."

"Fair enough, then your *rest and digest* mode is your internal spa treatment, which relaxes your mind and body from the inside."

"How is that?"

"James, imagine, you are running a marathon. You have put your blood and sweat in preparation for the race and now you are on the verge of winning it. The only hitch is that the runner in the second position is only seconds behind you, which means he can, at any time, overtake you. This makes your sympathetic, *fight or flight* mode go into overdrive. This means your heart is pumping out more blood and your lungs are breathing faster than ever before. There is extra sweat because of the added pressure on you to hold on to your first position. Now there are only seconds left as you inch closer to the finishing line. Your heart is pumping so fast that you feel it might just pop out of your body but you keep going on with your eyes fixed on the finish line. Seconds later, you go on to cross the finishing line and win the marathon."

"You lie down breathing out loud. Suddenly, you notice that there is a smile on your face, your breathing is slowing down and some of that sweat disappears. Your body is in the cooling-off mode. This is where your parasympathetic, *rest & digest* system starts kicking in. It releases neurochemicals and neurotransmitters, which slow down your system and relax your body and bring you back to a state of normalcy."

"That's a fantastic analogy, I took part in a couple of marathons in New York but never thought about my body undergoing any of this!"

"You see James I gave that analogy because life is a marathon, which you will keep running as long as you are alive. The day you take your last breath, that's the end of your life's marathon."

"Does this give you clarity on the point I earlier mentioned - breathing is the only voluntary function in the body which has the power to alter your involuntary functions?"

"Crystal clear."

"Breathing is the most important fuel for your body, which is necessary not just to survive but also to thrive."

"Just as regular physical exercises strengthen your physical endurance levels, if practiced properly, breathing strengthens your emotional endurance levels. If you regulate your breathing you can strengthen your internal world against any external threats."

That was quite an insight for James.

He spent the rest of the afternoon with other yogis and then went into the Ashram library. It was a treasure trove of information about spirituality and knowledge. He went through the various titles and also read the many real-life testimonies of people who narrated their eureka moments or transformation stories after their sojourn at the Ashram. The Ashram is host to people from all walks of life and all parts of the globe.

James had never bothered to read a single page beyond trading books, let alone a chapter in the huge stockpile of books in his fancy downtown office library. Nor did he play his life by the spiritual books. He believed in achieving success by hook or by crook.

A few years ago....

Someone was exhaling in a downtown office in New York. It was one posh corner office of Wall Street in Manhattan, New York. It overlooked the hundreds of skyscrapers, thousands of people who had millions of aspirations walking there every morning. Dark chocolate was always associated with indulgence and luxury. The furniture and upholstery in the cabin resembled the same rich taste, colour and quality of the finest dark chocolate. Though there was a stark difference compared to all the other organizations in the vicinity. Every morning the CEO started his day, sitting, not on a chair, but on a yoga mat. RK, as he was called, kick-started his day, in his cabin, by religiously focusing on breathing and it was not a solo act. The practice was followed by each and every member of his enterprise. The enterprise made millions with just this one practice. How? After all, the stress levels at the organization had dropped over 40% and so had the attrition rates, which had been costing the company millions. After all, a wise man once said, every penny saved is every penny earned. For RK, the enterprise, and corporate America, this was a breath of fresh air…

CHAPTER 12
Breathing is the Battery of Life

The Ashram was freshness personified! Guruji had invited James to one of the spaces in the Ashram called Asha. Asha meant hope. This space had a very trance-like feel, vivid colours splashed on the wall. A myriad lighting effects giving it a psychedelic feel. Plus, the sounds of nature coming in from the huge French windows on either side allowing cross ventilation plus sights and sounds of nature. There were the beautiful birds, Asian Koel and the Indian Robin competing with each other on either side of the windows.

James thought, 'in a few hours these birds will pack up for the night, fly into their nests only to come out full throttle, the next morning'. He wondered about the engineering of birds and what was their purpose on planet earth.

"Their purpose is to bring music to our ears, keep the planet clean of rodents and green for other species to thrive. I saw what you were looking at," Guruji interrupted James' thoughts.

"You are right again Guruji, I think I should just keep my eyes closed in front of you."

"Well, I don't need your eyes open to read them."

James smiled while looking at the him as he said, "Before you say anything else, I am ready to learn the breathing aspects of ancient times."

"But before we begin understanding about the breathing of ancient times, you need to have the right affirmations."

"And what are those?"

"Remember, breathing is the only voluntary function that can alter and transform your involuntary autonomic nervous system."

"I get that."

"James what if I told you that what the modern-day scientific community is discovering about breathing was already discovered at least a few thousands of years ago?"

"Are you sure?"

"Of course. Let me take you through a little time-lapse."

Guruji explained that breathing is associated with the word of life or spirit in various languages and cultures around the world. In ancient Sanskrit language, the word breathing is called 'Prana', which means life. The Hebrew texts mention the word 'Ruach', which means breath and spirit. If one looks at the ancient Latin texts, the word 'Spiritus' is defined as breath and spirit. In ancient Greek culture, 'Numa' has the same meaning. He further explained that the ancient cultures of the world knew a lot about this delicate nexus between life and breathing.

"That is so informative!"

"Yes James, humans were an intelligent race back then too. This brings me to another thought-provoking point. Tell me, were there X-Ray machines, ultrasound scanners or MRI machines back then, for humans to understand the central nervous system?"

"Not that I am aware of, why do you ask?"

"Simple. These so-called advanced machines can

investigate only the physical layer of humans. People back then understood the breathing faculty as a major component of life. If one learns and practices the art of breathing, then that person can regulate his or her emotions. This, in turn, enables better control of the involuntary, autonomic nervous system at the physical level."

"Really?" James went into his monologue mode - 'regulating breathing..., until now I only knew about regulating investment portfolios and being hounded by equity regulations in the stock market. I wonder what this means in terms of breathing...'?

"James, seems like you have gone back into your corporate days. Are you with me?"

"Oh yes, I am - but it is still not very clear."

"Very well, answer this simple question. What's common between cell phones, laptops, remote control, flashlights, electric cars, quartz watches, or even those old pocket calculators?"

"Wait a minute, are we not going to talk about breathing?"

"Yes, we are, but first answer the question."

"The fact that none of them can function without a battery."

"Exactly! That was fast."

"Knowledge is infectious, I guess."

"And how does a battery function?"

"It has a anode or the positive side and cathode, the negative side. So?" James was perplexed.

"Just like the two sides of a battery which keep your gadgets charged, there are two energies flowing through nature, which keep your breathing and life charged up 24/7. The answer lies in the ancient texts of Kundalini Yoga.

According to those texts, our bodies have been designed to let certain channels of energy flow into them. They are called *Nadis.*"

"There are two energies called 'Ida' and 'Pingla' that intertwines both sides of the spine and unite to form the 'Sushumna', the central channel. The Ida, is on the left nostril, the Pingla, is on the right nostril and Sushumna runs on the centre of the nose between the upper lip and the tip of the nose."

"The Ida is termed as moon energy, which symbolizes the characteristics of being cool, calm, collected and reflective. The Pingla represents the sun energy, which is known for being bright, fiery and awakening."

Guruji then showed James an image. "James, does this look familiar to you?"

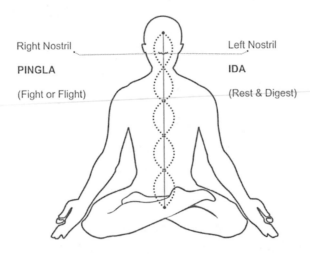

"Oh, yes, this is the same chart you had shown me while explaining the modern-day version of our nervous system.

But here I can see that Ida has replaced the Parasympathetic and Pingla has replaced the Sympathetic."

"Excellent James. Just like parasympathetic - Ida, the left nostril helps our nervous system get into the reflective and introspective mode. It activates the right side of your brain. This side of your brain is associated with creativity, passion, emotions, intuition and performance arts. At this stage, your body is in introvert mode and switches to functions of digestion, circulation, sleep cycle and helps it to relax and rejuvenate."

"Pingla, the right nostril helps the system to get active in the physical mode. It is responsible for activating the left side of your brain which is all about logic, language, reasoning, analysis and calculation Just like other forces in nature, one side is always more dominant than the other. Just imagine, the ancient yogis discovered the sympathetic and parasympathetic modes more than 5000 years ago."

But James was eager and impatient. "What happens in Sushumna?"

"That's a good question. Let me ask you, have you ever seen those old weighing scales that have two pans? The kind that is held by the blindfolded statue of Justice?"

"Yes, I have."

"Do you know what would happen if one side is more dominant on the weighing scale?"

"Yes, we will have to keep putting more weights to the scale to balance them."

"When both sides of the scale are in sync, it is the period of pure bliss. It is the desired state where your cognitive and creative juices are in balance. A state where rationale and emotions are in sync. It is the perfect harmony of physical and mental wellbeing. I would call it a state where you paint your own canvas. That's because you have total control over your thoughts and emotions."

"Let me give you an example. Normally when you close your eyes, you have various images running across them like a photo album. Each photo evokes a response either in terms of emotions or analysis. Some delight you while others you detest. This happens because one of your channels is dominant. Sushumna is the stage when this photo album is best enjoyed as pictures without any judgements, emotions or feelings. You would just enjoy each picture as it opens without analysing them. It's the ultimate stage of quiescence."

"During this stage, energy flows with perfect balance in a state of quiet self-observation. This is the meditative state. To achieve this state, one needs long and sustained practice."

"This is the state where your mind becomes a 'witness' in the detached mode to the happenings around you, without affecting you – giving one the enormous strength required to deal with any complex situation."

"I guess, it is easier said than done," a bemused James retorted.

"Yes, to achieve this state one requires long and sustained practice. James, tell me do you watch movies back home?"

"Yes, I am a big movie buff."

"When you watch a horror movie, do you let the ghosts of the movie play in your mind forever?"

"No, I go there for entertainment and leave them all at the movie theatre itself."

"See, you have answered your own question."

"Sushumna frees your mind of any ghosts. It allows you to play various life movies right in front of your eyes. Horror, war, serial killers, romance, mystery but it does not allow you to be affected anymore. You just watch it playing in front of your eyes but it does not touch or move you anymore. At this stage, your mind is a fortress and your arsenal of emotions are well preserved."

With James fighting plenty of internal battles, Guruji couldn't have given him a better analogy.

"You know what gets even better?" Guruji continued.

"What?"

"Your nostrils have a cycle, which means there is a shift between your left and right nostril every 60 to 120 minutes. Just like life itself, your breathing has a cycle too. Such is the brilliance of nature and human engineering. But, there is a very important ingredient which affects your breathing cycles."

"And that ingredient is?"

"Emotions."

"In ancient times, people had discovered and implemented the techniques of breathing to regulate emotions, maintaining their equilibrium at the physical layer."

"So, this means that one has to regulate emotions to keep equilibrium at the physical layer?"

"That's the word, James, just like you regulate the gas on the stove to cook your food, you need to regulate your breathing patterns to control your emotions and thus enjoy the maximum flavours of life. It is also important to keep a check on the various sources of inputs – so as to avoid generating emotions which can trigger Pingla, the *fight or flight* mode."

"What breathing does to emotional endurance levels is exactly as gaining physical endurance by doing regular physical exercises. People, back in ancient times, understood the significance of the breathing faculty as a major component of life, to regulate their emotions and control their physical layers."

"Wow, never imagined that breathing, so simple is so powerful."

"Yes, James. While we don't see tigers or lions on our streets to activate our *fight or flight* mode, our modern-day lifestyle of *habit-to-compare* and constantly running after *'what-we-don't-have'* has become key to putting our bodies in a continuous *fight or flight* mode. This does not let our *rest & digest* system activate itself. As a result, common lifestyle diseases like anxiety, depression, blood pressure, obesity, cardiovascular problems and other illnesses become prevalent."

"The *rest and digest* system is your internal spa treatment which relaxes your mind and body from the inside. If you have regulated your breathing, you can strengthen your internal, emotional world, against any external threats. But this is achieved only with time and the right tools."

"Right tools?"

"Yes, the right tools. You can drive a car in low gear but is your engine going to be efficient? It will break down sooner or later. Isn't it? Similarly, to make your breathing efficient and perform at maximum mileage, you will have to use the right tools and the right techniques."

"And how do you do that?"

"Before I tell you how to do it, I want you to put some theory into practice. Go jog five rounds of the Ashram and let's reconvene after you sweat it out and then in the shower, reflect on what has been said. Your *fight or flight* and *rest and digest* system will come into play. Ready, steady, go."

James had not jogged in a long time, and today's jog would put a great deal of pressure on his physical, physiological and psychological levels, but he was prepared for it. He had never imagined that the function of breathing was so simple yet so powerful, which could impact the entire autonomic nervous system of the body.

Guruji had asked him to meet after exactly 60 minutes, therefore, he had no more time to think, he just began taking deep breaths...

A few years ago

Breathe in. Now breathe out, RK told himself. Breathing always helped him gather his emotions and thoughts before he took any major decisions. Today, he was about to have a meeting with the senior leadership of the enterprise. My opening remarks are going to be – "I have a formula…"

CHAPTER 13
Breathing *Four-mula*

James was breathing hard and heavy as he jogged along the Nirvana area of the Ashram.

He put the voluntary function of breathing through several tests. Be it the exhaustive panting while taking five rounds of the Ashram or his relaxed breathing pattern while the water spray made its way from the showerhead to his skin. He even felt it while closing his eyes for five minutes after getting dressed. In having done this he noticed that the people around him had an upbeat mood while chatting him up. He met a former scientist from the USA, a former gangster from Brazil and a permaculture specialist from China. James was taken aback at the diverse backgrounds of these people. This Ashram looked as if it was sowing different seeds in the huge garden of Eden.

James heard a voice from behind, "Exactly 59 minutes and 26 seconds. James that's fantastic. You are putting practicality and punctuality to good use. Looks like the breathing session was a breath of fresh air to you. Thankfully, we are just getting started. Are you ready for another session?"

"Ever ready!" James replied.

"Look at you, the same James who was feeling irritated at closing his eyes for even two minutes that first day, to a person who has stuck by me for days now."

"It proves that every sceptic needs the right Guru to believe in."

"Glad to know that. So, shall we?"

"Yes, I am ready to learn the breathing techniques."

"Before we begin the most powerful techniques of ancient breathing, you need to have the right assertions."

"And what is that Guruji?"

"Breathing is the only voluntary function that can alter and transform your autonomic nervous system."

"Oh, of course, that was pretty much clear in the last two sessions."

"Ok, tell me James, what formula comes to mind when I mention the name, 'Einstein'?"

"$E=mc^2$ Guruji but why do you ask, I thought this class is on breathing techniques and not physics."

"Well, James. human engineering is a lot about physics as we have mentioned, be it your physical or anatomical layer. Nevertheless, what I am about to tell you is a formula that you will never forget when it comes to breathing."

"Hopefully, it's a lot easier than Einstein's formula."

"Absolutely! It's no rocket-science." was the quirky response from Guruji.

"This formula is called *Four-mula.*"

Guruji drew a quick chart:

- *Four squared* – breathing exercise to Calm down
- *Fourtify* - breathing exercise to Charge up

"James, the above two bring into rhythm the Parasympathetic and Sympathetic sides of our Autonomic nervous system. Do you recall them from our earlier conversations?"

"Yes, I do,"

"Excellent!"

Guruji continued, "Let's now get to the breathing exercise for calming emotions. I call this *'Four squared'*."

"Any guesses James on this name?"

"Yes, I know it has something to do with the number 4."

"That's great. Yes, it has something to do with the number 4. So, let's not waste 4 more seconds on this. Here's how you can crack the *fourmula*."

This is one formula I am looking to crack. James had seen plenty of formulas, algorithms and equations in the stock market. This was a welcome change.

"Are you ready James?"

"Never been more," James retorted in seconds.

"Ok, James, first breathe in with a count of four."

James went down memory lane where he would take a long drag of pot for four to five seconds just to relieve the onslaught of the markets on his mind.

"Now hold your breath for four seconds."

Those four seconds, seemed like an eternity to James. He remembered how he used to tell everyone in his team that every second matters on the trading floor and yet here he was counting his breaths for 4 seconds wondering whether this was even worth it.

"James, you are investing time so this is all going to be worth it."

'There it goes, Guruji's telepathic mind, he caught me out yet again', James soliloquised.

"Now exhale for a count of four, James."

The last time James exhaled loudly was probably when he was reflecting on his life at the hospital after the car crash.

"James, initially you will feel the skeletons emerging from deep within your thoughts but it is not that bad. Hold your thoughts for the first four seconds."

"Guruji, this is a lot more difficult than I expected."

"My dear James, this exercise teaches you one thing."

"And what's that Guruji?"

"Nothing comes easy nor can anything be taken for granted in life. Not even breathing. Come on James, it's simple. Train your breaths harder. Breathe in and count to four. Hold and count to four. Exhale and count to four. Rest for another four. To start with, do this exercise for 4 minutes."

James began to put those words into action using the chart as his guide.

"What are you feeling James?"

"A lot calmer and more reflective than I was four minutes ago."

"That is a good observation James."

"This exercise triggers your *rest and digest mode*, improves your parasympathetic nervous system, and blood circulation. An excellent technique for those suffering from hypertension and cardiovascular disorders. What's even better? It can be done anywhere and at any time."

"That's easy."

"It's not unless you follow a system."

"What does that system involve?"

"Sitting cross-legged, eyes closed and arms on your knees. For those who can't sit in this position, you can sit on a chair and keep your arms on your knees. The key is to keep your back straight. Do this exercise for 4 minutes at a time for the first few days, and then increase it gradually as you practice."

"What else does this do, Guruji?"

"Apart from regulating the autonomic nervous system, it also stabilizes your body temperature and blood pressure. Plus, it prevents mental illnesses like depression, panic disorder and anxiety problems." So, one breath is all it takes. Inhale optimism, exhale pessimism. *Fourmula* is your formula for life's deepest answers.

"And James, ready for the next one?"

"Ever ready!"

"Good, but before that, tell me, have you seen Usain Bolt run?"

"Of course, who hasn't?"

"Well James, if you have, then you will know he runs in short bursts that is quite literally like striking bolt of lightning."

"Now, why are we talking about running?"

"To make you understand about activating your breath. I also call this exercise *'fourtify'* that is **F O U R T I F Y**." *Guruji stressed each alphabet.*

"Guruji, again I see this has something to do with Four."

"Yes, it does, but there's a lot more. The word stands for number four and forty. Plus, it also symbolizes the word fortify, which means 'to strengthen'. This exercise charges your system and gets your *fight or flight,* sympathetic nervous system up and running. In this case, you will be producing short bursts of energy to win any task at hand. James, have you watched a 100m race at the Olympics?"

"Oh! Yes, I have Guruji, why?"

"Consider this next exercise as a mix of running, jogging and walking. Inhale-and-exhale four times. This is the stage when your body is slowly warming up before you get started."

James began to breathe in and out and felt as if a heavy weight on his chest was choking him. James could think of the four-letter word that started with F. "This is hard Guruji."

- "Next, you exhale 40 times quickly and non-stop. This is like the 100m sprint where you are huffing and puffing to win the race.
- After this, again perform the long inhale-exhale breath 4 times.

Exhale 40 times again, hard and fast through your belly. "Repeat this cycle. To start with, do this for 4 minutes at a time for the initial few days, and then, as you practice, increase it gradually up to 14 minutes."

"The important thing here is to activate breathing from your belly and not just from your lungs. Till you don't reach the belly, breathing will not activate your concentric layers nor your sympathetic system. Another important tip, do this first thing in the morning on an empty stomach to kick-start your day. You can say goodbye to that cup of coffee in the morning as this exercise will have effects that are stronger than caffeine and without any side effects."

"Oh no, there goes my cup of coffee," James remarked in a sarcastic tone.

"James, you can brew a whole new approach towards your work with this one exercise. Follow the system as told. During the first exercise - sit cross-legged with your eyes closed and place each arm on both sides of the knee or sit on a chair and keep your arms on your knees. The key is to keep your back straight. Now make a circle with your fingers by placing your index finger in your thumb. While doing this exercise, keep a positive vibe and energy around you."

"To start with, do this exercise for 4 minutes, and increase it gradually as you practice."

"What are the benefits that I will experience after this exercise?"

"Ah, James there are plenty of them but just to mention a few, your concentration and decision-making skills will touch a new high. You will become self-confident, positive and more affirmative in your personal and professional life. Plus, it improves mental alertness and agility. For a fitness-conscious person like you, this exercise will help you lose weight and improve digestion. Start using this technique not more than twice a day. After a few weeks of regular practice, you can increase it to three times or so. However, remember this important point – this exercise should be done either on an empty stomach or at least with a gap of two hours after eating. Do you want to try it now?"

"Yes, I do."

"Great, try it and let me know how you feel."

James did the exercise and felt as though he had been given an injection of steroids. He felt a boost of energy all through his body and a crystal-clear clarity in his thoughts. He felt he was ready to go home and undo all the wrong things he had done in his life.

James was craving many things. To go back to New York. To try to reunite with his ex. To put all the controversies behind him.

"Don't even think of going back home James, not at the moment," came Guruji's voice. It was uncanny how he could read what James had in his mind.

"James looking at you, I can say you were not short of money, fame and powerful people around you. Though you have always been short of one basic ingredient."

"What is that Guruji?"

"Focus on breathing, and be with your own thoughts. And, for the coming days, do as I say…."

James took a deep breath…

A few years ago

There was an upbeat mood in the markets but the same mood could not be felt in RK's workforce. The team felt that their jobs were hanging in the air and the day would not be far when they are shown the dreaded 'pink slip'.

Today was a crucial meeting with the senior management regarding the fate of several employees. At the meeting he was shown the bottom lines of the balance sheets which were all in red, hitting new lows. He saw the red arrows on the presentation running in front of him. As each slide passed by, the picture kept looking grimmer and grimmer. Even then, RK was unflappable and went through each slide with a sense of tranquility. He advised his team to research not only the data and numbers but to come up with workable solutions as well.

CHAPTER 14
James is back!

Something disruptive was playing crystal-clear in James' mind on a cloudy, misty morning at the Ashram. The sun was trying to play hide and seek with the environs. The leaves were rustling in the gentle breeze. The birds provided a beautiful chorus in the background. All this didn't matter to one person sitting under a tree. His eyes were shut tight. He was motionless in his actions but his thoughts were tumbling in his mind, thick and fast. All this while in the past, James had his focus on money, fame, women and business. He had no idea that the most elementary thing in the world would be the most difficult to grasp. That is, to concentrate on your breathing pattern, and become aware of your own thoughts. It seemed the toughest job in the world for him.

Guruji had asked him to practice the breathing techniques for a week, but to him, it felt like a millennium. It felt as if he was held captive in an inescapable prison - his mind.

It's one thing to learn techniques, but a very different thing to put them into practice. He was in solo mode for a week, reclusive to everyone in the Ashram yet inclusive in his own thoughts. In the past, James had always craved the spotlight and centre-stage where he could play the role of a brilliant manipulator with effortless artistry. Now he had no stage, no actors to play with, no spotlight, no audience. *Just silence and his thoughts.*

The first two days were difficult trying to master the techniques but things began to change dramatically, much like dark clouds clearing up in the blue skies above. The clouds were gone and so were his doubts. With every breath, his mind became more focused and more tranquil. He was trying to control his breathing, techniques which were a mix of slow and rapid breaths. James never felt so connected to his thoughts. The seeds of Guruji's teachings were beginning to sprout.

While James was respiring in the air of equanimity, on the other side of the world, someone was suspiring as though he had been hit on his chest with a brick. It was Stephen, a member of the Board of Directors of Neo Industries. He felt defeated and angered by the disappearance of James Hatman. It was a pressure-cooker situation for the company, as the media, law enforcement and other stakeholders were at a war of words. Nobody knew how James had slipped out of America without a trace. That was just one part of the problem for trouble was exploding from all corners like the demolition of a building with dynamite.

Rumours were surfacing that there had been a huge cover-up about the Neo scandal. There were also reports coming in that Neo was riddled with corruption at various levels. One report even suggested that James was just a scapegoat for the entire rotten system that was in place.

There was someone else who was breathing with resentment. Her enigmatic eyes had this gloomy look and her rose-pink cheeks had turned pale. James was a thing of the past for Eliza, yet there was a connection between them.

'Alas, if only I had been with him, maybe all this could have been avoided', said her heart. Yet, the mind was in total conflict. *'This was bound to happen, he called for it. Karma comes to haunt you sooner or later. He treated you and others like shit. Stop being sorry for him, cheer up'.* This war had her in self-destruction mode.

The CIA, FBI and Department of Treasury were all on a manhunt for James. So far, they had no formal arrest warrants as the ongoing investigations were not enough to label him but he was the critical link to the happenings of the company.

Another office was witnessing a lot of action. That was the office of James' law team, spearheaded by JJ. They were busy preparing press statements and defence briefs for James. It was probably one of the toughest jobs in America right now, but if there was one man who could pull it off, JJ was the perfect fit.

While all this was happening, JJ looked for a handkerchief in his suit pocket. While he flipped out the handkerchief something fell out. A flash drive, the USB read: 'from James'. JJ was zapped for a moment. How in hell was this possible? Did someone just play a prank on him? He had a grin on his face that attested to the fact that James had always been one step ahead of everyone else.

JJ plugged in the USB device to his laptop and a video began playing. With every second that passed, his eyes opened wider and his smile got broader. His entire office saw the look of glee on his face. He said, "ladies and gentlemen, we have just found our most potent defence, James himself! Call for a press conference at 4 this evening". JJ exhaled loudly and muttered: *James, where are you, man? Wherever you are, hope you are well, just hang in there'.*

James was smoothly breathing and becoming aware of

his thoughts. Suddenly, his mind replayed his encounter with JJ at the hospital. It was there, when he hugged JJ, that he had quietly slipped that flash drive into JJ's pocket. Perhaps, James being the visionary had seen this day coming. He needed the armour in his defence just in case things got bad. James had whispered in his mind: *'JJ I have placed everything in there, over to you now'.*

After dinner, everybody at the Ashram was dispersing to retire for the night. James made a gesture to everyone with a finger on his lips, which meant he had gone into silence mode. Not everyone understood this gesture but they gave him space and time.

On the other side of the world, the reporters were coming together for the press conference, slated to be held at 4 pm. The moment finally arrived and as the clock struck 4, JJ greeted the Press: "Ladies and gentlemen, good evening. It's my pleasure to make a few announcements. Actually I will not be doing that. James is going to do it himself. The press went into a frenzy: Are you kidding, is James here? What? James is here?"

It was as if Breaking News had begun flashing on their screens. Nobody could believe it as reporters shouted: Is James here?

JJ said, "Yes, indeed he is". The press went berserk as soon as they heard this. Then JJ said, "Though there are some changes in plans. James is on the screen."

And the video began to play.

"Ladies and Gentlemen if you are watching this; I might not be there amongst you. Rest assured; I am not a fugitive. I am not running away nor do I have anything to hide. I was a problem child for my parents even as an adult. But if there is one thing that I have learnt from them it is to stand up and tell the truth. That is what I am doing today. I would like to say sorry to the entire Neo Industries team for this tragedy that took place. I am sorry for the victim, his family and everyone involved. At the same time, I would like to clarify that I had nothing to do with this accident. According to my psychologist, I am suffering from severe Post Traumatic Stress Disorder. Staying there in the thick of things would have made me lose my sanity or go into depression. That's the last thing I want right now with so much on my plate. I wanted to gather my thoughts and return greater and stronger. I repeat, I am not running away from anything – the day you have any conclusive evidence against me, I will be standing right before your eyes instead of talking through this video. I will be watching the developments and proceedings very closely. Nobody knows where I am, at least not yet, so I request you all not to hound my legal team, especially JJ who has stood by me through thick and thin. They are doing an outstanding job and I know by the time I am back; JJ and team would have been able to piece this puzzle together. Once again, I request you all to respect my privacy, space and time. See you all very soon."

The press was quiet as reporters began their analysis. While some of them empathized with James, the others were still relentless and called him an absconder.

While all this was happening, James' phone buzzed on the other side of the world. It was early morning and a new notification showed up on his phone. As he read it, he murmured, 'Thanks JJ. You chose the right moment and stage to sow the first seed towards proof of my innocence'.

A few years ago...

RK *called for a video conference with all employees around the world. He was to make some key announcements. Given the tough market situation, this conference call had sent shivers up the spines of many employees who were anticipating it to be an announcement for workforce cut and pink-slips for many.*

However, as the call started, RK spoke – "Dear team, we all know the current tough economic times. The easy route for me is to reduce costs by cutting the workforce. But I do not want to do that. I believe in each one you."

He continued, "Today I have decided to take a cut of 50% in my salary. I have requested a 20% pay cut from my senior leadership, and will put in place a 5% cut in the salaries of the remaining workforce. This would mean that I can continue to ride this ship, and ensure enough lifeboats are available for my entire workforce. As your Captain I hope you all will accept my decision."

His decision went down very well across the ranks of the entire company. There wasn't a single resignation. On the contrary, the workforce was more determined than ever to turn around the fortunes of the company under his leadership.

CHAPTER 15
Choices & the Kernel

C is for Choices

In the principle of Cause-Effect, Choice is the Cause;

You control Choice before you exercise it, thereafter, Choice controls you;

Choice is the boon endowed only to Humans but many consider it a bane;

More people in this world are hurt by the incorrect Choice of words than in a war;

Choose what you say rather than say what you Choose;

As you grow in life, personal or professional – importance of making the right Choice takes centre stage;

The good, the bad and the ugly. Choose how you want to start your day;

You are just a Choice away from success or failure.

Making a Choice is an attitude.

James was fascinated reading all these quotes in the corridor just before walking into the room called Vichinta, meaning 'Reflections'. He was here that, after a week of reclusion practicing breathing exercises and becoming aware of his thoughts. Now he was about to get his next question solved about something he was not very proud of – *Choices*. Curiosity getting the better of him James had asked this question in his previous session. Guruji had politely reminded him about the right time and place. So, here he was, looking at the external world with his eyes reading those quotes, which created a stirring up of emotions within him. The sun was setting in the far distance but the thoughts in his head were dawning with clarity day by day.

"James, I can feel that you are excited about our very next session, a topic you had raised earlier. Tell me, James, what is your favourite dish or cuisine? Do you have any favourite cuisine or Indian food that you love?"

"For some reason I love Dal Makhani."

"Oh, I was expecting you to say butter chicken or chicken tikka but I am glad you love plant-based Indian food too." "Tell me one thing, do you go to a cow and ask whether it would like to have Dal Makhani or Pasta today?"

"Wait, are you serious?"

"You bet I am. Now answer the question."

"No, obviously not. The cow eats what it gets, which is mostly raw grass and other leafy greens."

"What about the tiger, can you tell the tiger in the jungle to stop hunting as you have chicken tikka to feed it?"

"No, you can't. A tiger will hunt its prey unless you keep it in a zoo and feed it, but the basic instinct of the tiger will not change," James replied.

"Great and do you think the Bengal tiger likes hunting and the African tiger likes to chill and not hunt?"

"No, be it the Bengal, African or Siberian tiger, you cannot take away the basic traits of the species. It's like taking out the Dal from Dal Makhani or the chicken from the chicken tikka."

"Well said, James, I feel you are getting hungry as dinner time approaches but let these thoughts slowly cook in your head. Just for your information, chicken tikka won't be served here. Dal yes, but not the makhani."

James had a smile on his face. "I'll take anything here, the food here is yum - even the dishes with very little spices, they turn out tasting delicious."

"Rather I would say we have the right spices when it comes to food and learning," Guruji retorted.

Dinner was wholesome and scrumptious. James thoroughly enjoyed the dal, Indian lentils and green vegetables along with chapattis, the Indian style cooked bread. But questions were still popping up in his head about the 'choices' conversation which he had with Guruji so far.

James was beginning to feel that he was going to unravel some unique facets about choice, which he was not yet aware of. The *ABCD* journey of learning was taking his awareness levels and his outlook on life towards a beautiful and colourful spectrum. He was resonating more and more with the ROYGBIV rainbow colours and seven concentric layers of human engineering.

"So, how was dinner?"

"Oh Guruji, the awareness strengthening exercises seem to be really working on my taste buds. I was becoming aware to every ingredient and every spice added to the food as soon as I started eating. The food was just delicious and yum."

"Looks like breathing exercises too. Your sense of humour is also getting flavourful and rhythmic." Now let's get back to business.

"James back home, did you have a choice to go to a fancy restaurant on a date or to order fast-food delivery when you were tired?"

"Oh, yes – umpteen times, both fancy restaurants and ordering in fast food. I do love cooking but seldom get the time for it."

"I presume you have the choice to order whatever you want to eat, correct?"

"Yes, I do."

"Why am I asking you all these questions James? It is because I am trying to make you understand that only humans as a race have a choice in not just what we want to eat but anything we want to do." "This is a boon which has been given to mankind. Unfortunately, many of us consider it a bane."

"Means animals and birds don't have such choices?"

"Yes, choice is the faculty which puts humans above all other species on the planet. Only humans have been endowed with choice as an option in everything we do. Animals have to live their lives in a certain defined and pre-programmed way."

"Guruji, could you make it simpler?"

"The most simple way to understand the choice faculty is to know that it is a cause and effect' relationship. You reap what you sow. If I were to refine it further, the cause and effect in our lives happen because of the choices we make. The choices I make today will impact me the very next second, minute, year or even decade later. Fair enough?"

"Now the next question is: why do we make certain choices in life? Can you think of one line or rather one word?"

"Fate or destiny maybe."

"Again James, you are talking of external factors when

the answer lies within. It is indeed your *kernel*, the seed layer – the sixth layer in the seven wonders of human engineering."

"The kernel layer…how?"

"You see James, kernel is the intrinsic component in human engineering which manifests as thoughts and desires at intellectual and emotional layers. It further translates as actions at the physical layer."

"Seems to go over my head. Please could you explain it to me in simpler terms?"

"James, have you ever seen a filament?"

"Of course, it's the integral part of a light bulb."

"Right, now a filament is present in a lamp, tube light, water heater or an air conditioner, agreed? So, what's the difference, James?"

"Its form."

"Correct, in a lamp, the filament produces yellow light, in a tube light it is white, in a water heater it produces heat and, in a refrigerator, it cools down the temperature. The source of all these devices is electricity but in all these examples, the filament is changing the electrical energy into different forms."

"So, where do cause and effect come into all of this?"

"Imagine the filament to be your kernel, the seed personality, and the electricity to be your soul or *Atman*. The light from *Atman* manifests via *kernel* as thoughts at Intellect layer and desires at Emotional layer, and further translates as actions at the Physical layer."

"Remember James, on the first day I told you about the kernel, the seed personality the sixth layer in our seven concentric layers. That is why I said, two siblings can grow up to take up two distinct careers. One as a police officer and the other as a dacoit or terrorist. It's the seed layer which causes you to make choices in life. So, if your seed layer is filled with positive vibes and influences, thus will be your thoughts and emotions in life, and vice versa."

"'Wow, that filament example did light up the bulb in my mind. This man just continues to fascinate me', James muttered."

"Guruji, thanks for throwing light on this topic, quite literally but if I may, could I add another question to this observation?"

"I am all ears."

"Don't you feel if the seed layer was pre-programmed for humans then what would make us different from animals?"

"Great question James. I have an excellent tale to tell you about Gautam Buddha. It's about this famous dacoit Angulimaala, a murderous dacoit, who used to cut the fingers off of his victims and weave them into a garland which he wore around his neck. He killed at will and soon became the most feared man in that area. One day while he was passing a forest, he met Gautam Buddha who was sitting by a tree. He locked his eyes on the Sage as he thought that he had just found his next victim."

"Approaching Buddha, he asked 'Aren't you afraid of me, I am the most feared man in the entire state. I am the most powerful man in this kingdom. Now it is your turn to die'."

"Buddha replied that his mind did not fear death. Instead, he readily agreed to be Angulimaala's next victim provided he could cut a small branch from the tree. Angulimaala smiled and told him that it was not a big deal for the most powerful man and so he cut a branch with some leaves on it. Buddha was delighted to see this and then he asked him to go and fix the branch back onto the tree. Angulimaala asked Buddha whether he was joking. He said how can one fix a broken branch or leaves back to the tree? They are already dead. That's when the great Sage said, 'Angulimaala, you can take someone's life in a second but you cannot bring anyone back to life even if it takes a lifetime."

"'So how are you the most powerful person when you don't have the power to bring life to people. If you cannot bring people back to life, you have no right to take their life in the first place'. This one line made Angulimaala realise his mistake and drop his weapons for good. Not just that, he went on to become one of the most devoted disciples of the Buddha."

"Any learnings from this story James?"

"No matter how corrupted your seed kernel layer is, there is always a chance of reprogramming it. A trait only we humans have."

"Beautifully put James. It's never too late to reformat your hard disk."

James knew that he had plenty of choices to make once he headed home. Though his choices had been like the night sky so far, he could start afresh like the sunrise every morning. And so, he did.

A few years ago

The team reworked the data and numbers. They presented possible solutions too but the business scenario was still bleak in view of the very weak order bookings and pipeline.

Towards the end of the meeting, RK's senior management team sought his approval for downsizing, showing him the headcount numbers.

He had only one line for them, "Guys, today when our backs are against the wall, should I turn my back on my people? Not a chance. We have seen worse. I have a plan that will help us get back to our A-game."

CHAPTER 16
You are what you choose

It was seven in the morning. James was taking a jog downhill enjoying the scenic panorama and vistas of the Ashram. He reached the local market and was seduced immediately by the plethora of colours, traditions and cultures running like a current, within the community. There was so much brilliance in the various handicrafts which fused excellently with the flavours of the fresh ground spices in the various shops around town. Some of the spices would wind up in large cartons to be exported, while others would make their way into the various kitchens of the local eateries and homes in the area.

The tangible fragrance of the peppers, piquancy of the tamarind chutney and zest of the chilli powder gave James a heady rush. All of these ingredients were making their way into the various popular Indian snacks like samosas and kachoris. He could no longer resist their pull. He sat down at one of the local joints and got down to business.

As he sat down, he couldn't help noticing the nearby cows which were being fed by a local villager. The cow has garnered a great deal of significance over the years in India as it is thought to be the symbolism of civilization, agriculture and religion. James was observing something more than what he used to see in the past. Learning and practicing the *A & B* of the *ABCD* program had raised his awareness to a new level and had added rhythm to his breathing. He was so fascinated by the ambience around him that he decided to stay there all day. He noticed how cows were pre-programmed to eat-sleep-milk-repeat mode. It appeared as if a defined set of tasks had been written and assigned to them. They did not seem to possess the intellect layer to choose something other than their natural engineering system. Humans, perhaps, are the only species who can make choices and write their own programs.

"Very well put James," Guruji said when James was back at the Ashram for his next session.

"All thanks to evolution and our intellect layer, this is the most precious gift that has given to humans. This layer enables humans to think, judge and make their own decisions. We might be compromised in terms of our physical size compared to animals but our intellect has certainly outmanoeuvred other species. So much so we use animals to create industries out of like animal husbandry, dairy and meat. I don't endorse the killing of animals or treating them with disdain and holding them in appalling conditions but sadly that's the reality of commercialization."

"Our mental strength has overpowered their physical strength. Just consider this, according to WWF (World Wide Fund for nature) earth has lost nearly half of its wildlife in the past 40 years."

"That's a shame!"

"James, we can undo and alter our reality every day and that's the beauty of waking up as the most intelligent species on earth. It's a shame our choices are degrading the environment and the communities around us. You don't need to be a Neil Armstrong and take a giant leap for mankind by landing on the moon. It's all about making small choices which can be a giant leap for your personality."

"What are those choices?" James was totally hooked.

"Though there are a million choices you could make - some of them could be as small as waking up early in the morning and going for a jog or hitting the snooze button and going back to slumberland. Another one could be liking, sharing or commenting on social media rather than working in the office. You have the choice to laze around and watch television or go for a weekend seminar on art, science or management. You can choose between a burger and a salad. You can choose to ignore and look the other way or protect someone who is being harassed in front of you."

"Whatever choices we make our human architecture, particularly our *kernel,* the seed layer is responsible for it. Do you remember James, I had earlier given you the example of the cow and tiger? Well, there's more to it."

"Even I need more clarity!"

"James, I told you that a tiger is pre-programmed to indulge in certain behaviours - be it an African Tiger, a Bengal Tiger or a Siberian Tiger. That's because animals have a *collective kernel,* whereas, Humans have *individual kernels.*"

"Because of the *collective* seed layer, the kernel – all animals in different categories i.e. all tigers or all cows or all horses etc., are bound to behave in similar ways vis-à-vis every human having *individualistic* seed layer, the kernel. That means you and I, unlike animals, will react differently to any situation and emotion."

"Ok, let me make it even simpler. Have you heard the

nursery rhyme 'Jack and Jill went up the hill'?"

"Yes, that's a classic."

"Now if I were to give a modern twist to this nursery rhyme and ask you to fill in the blanks with your interpretation other than the nursery rhyme, what would it be? Wait, let me write it down."

Guruji wrote in on a piece of paper – 'Jack and Jill went up the hill'… "James if I were to give you five minutes to write a story about what happened between Jack and Jill, it will perhaps be way different from mine. That's how the *individualistic* kernel works. Each human being, therefore, possesses distinct characteristics, each different from the other. This is the primary reason why a Manager, leading a team of humans, is paid higher than a circus ring master controlling a group of tigers."

"That analogy is so simple and true, yet so very, very powerful!" James was awe struck.

"Even the physical layer of animals has limitations vis-à-vis humans, when it comes to choices and flexibility. The design of the cow's physical layer i.e. anatomical and physiological – right from the dental anatomy to digestive system is designed to eat grass and leafy food only. The tooth structure of the cow is flat, designed to grind and chew only grass and leaves. It is not designed to tear flesh or grind bones. Their digestive system is designed to digest vegetation food alone, not meat."

"Similarly, the tooth structure of a tiger and other carnivore animals are sharp and have been designed to tear up flesh and grind bones, not to chew grass. Their digestive system is also designed to absorb meat and flesh with ease, but not greens or veggies."

"If you feed a tiger with grass for a long period, it will not survive. Similarly, if a cow is fed with meat for a long duration, it too will not survive."

"However, humans can make that choice between eating greens, veggies or meat. Our teeth and intestines have been engineered to eat and digest both. "A carnivore's body cools down by panting whereas an herbivore's body cools down by sweating. Now when you take humans into the equation who are omnivores by nature, we sweat and pant to cool our bodies down."

It was not just an eye-opener but also a revelation for James, as he had never given a thought to this perspective.

"Guruji, I have made decisions in the past which I now regret."

"I know James, but the best part is that you can undo all those mistakes by starting afresh like Angulimaala. You need to practice before a big game, right? You have to put time and effort into a relationship, correct? It starts from putting time into your *A, B* and *C*. Awareness helps you fortify your intellect level. Breathing regulates your emotional persona, which leads to better choices. For this *A, B* and *C* to flow seamlessly, you'll need *D* – Discipline to create a cycle of better decisions and emotions in life."

"Absolutely, you couldn't have put it better."

"James, that's why leadership and choices go hand-in-hand. One wrong choice and you could affect thousands of lives and millions of dollars."

This has been beautifully encapsulated in few lines during oriental times:

"When the vision is one year, cultivate flowers
When the vision is ten years, cultivate trees
When the vision is an eternity, cultivate people."

A few years ago...

RK *came out for the press conference, "Today I have made a tough choice but it's - the right one. My people have given their all to this company, sweat, blood and everything in between. So, I consider them not just employees but my Partners-In-Progress. That's why as the CEO and President of the company I am announcing a special ESOP (Employee stock option) for every employee of this company, which includes not just the senior leadership but every permanent employee of this company.*

"In addition to that, I have also got the Board to release $10 million to create a first-of-its-kind fund towards an innovation centre for learning and development. It will enable all those who want to keep up with and hone their learning and innovative skills."

With the announcement came rousing applause and a standing ovation for RK, *which lasted for nearly 30 minutes after he left the venue. It was time to think ahead of the curve, into the future....*

CHAPTER 17
Moving forward by looking back

James was retiring to his room for the night. For the first time in days, he switched on his phone though he kept his network switched off. All he wanted to do tonight was to look at some of the people who mattered the most to him. People he had loved, hated, hurt, wronged or deceived. As he looked at the gallery on his phone, the first album shot a current of happiness through him bringing with it a dollop of nostalgia. He was looking at pictures from his childhood. The first few pictures brought a smile to his face but then a second later a somber look took its place. The lines in his forehead were tense, his eyelids twitched and he could feel the buildup of teardrops as he looked at the picture of his parents.

A choice he had made years ago, which he regretted to this day. Leaving his home after a bitter tiff with his parents. He had decided to skip college and start something of his own. A decision which did not go down too well with his father. There were tiffs, squabbles and a feeling of unease between the two. Sandwiched between them was his poor mother who didn't know which way to turn. One final day the blitzkrieg reached its zenith when his father tossed him and his stuff out of the house. Instead of apologizing and trying to make amends, James had chosen to walk out. It was the choice he made that day.

Even when he became successful, he still had all that anger suppressed inside him. James just wanted to prove a point to his father about his net-worth so he kept on accumulating wealth and assets. Sadly, the reality was that his father was looking for only one asset, the return of his son and his time for his father.

They say time heals everything. It only does when two people make an effort during that time. Even though James' father did regret his decision to throw his son out of the house, James was in some sort of a redemption mode trying to reclaim his life and become the poster boy of the corporate world in New York's Wall Street.

When James became aware of his feelings for his parents, he decided to visit them. Sadly, it was too late as he entered the house only to find his father asking him who he was. No, his father wasn't being sarcastic or rude to him, it was a straightforward case of Dementia, which was triggered the day James left the house. What an irony, the father who wanted to forget his son after throwing him out, couldn't even remember him when he came back one fine day.

"Happy my son, seeing him like this? You never remembered us all these years, I guess karma has come back to haunt you."

James had tears in his eyes and fell to his knees and begged for forgiveness from his mom. In return, his dad could only ask, "Who is this young man? Why is he crying? Son where is your father? Have you seen him lately?"

Out of guilt, from that day onwards, he began sending

money for his father's treatment. He even recommended some of the best neurologists in the country. His mother forgave him but did not forget the pain James had put them through all those years by being an escapist and absent from their lives.

With every photo he flipped in his album, he regretted more and more the choices he had made with regard to his parents. He wanted to re-live each moment. He knew what he had to do once he got back. He had made a choice.

There was someone else he had turned his back on – Eliza. The woman with whom he had a whirlwind romance and which took the media by storm. She was the one who had stood by him through thick and thin. Yet, he disappeared out of thin air from her life leaving Eliza shedding untold tears. She had called him a narcissist and materialist the day she walked out of his office and his life. In hindsight, her choice of words was apt for him. He deserved her angst and hot temper for he had turned stone-cold towards her feelings.

'If only I had some time machine to go back to that day and apologize to her for what I had said', James mused.

He regretted the choice of using those harsh words when he told her that she has no identity of her own and that everyone knows her as being James Hatman's girlfriend. In fact, after leaving him, she had become a movie star and overshadowed her very persona in the media and entertainment circles. He had no stable girlfriend since then. Just a few flings and one-night stands.

Though he was a hotshot investment banker, he had never invested wisely in relationships. That's why his love treasury was as empty as his materialistic life back home. This investment did not require his riches or flamboyant lifestyle, just two things, time and effort from his side for Eliza. Unfortunately, he gave none and after Eliza, he had lost the patience to invest in anything that needed an emotional transaction.

'I need to make one last settlement with Eliza', James decided.

The only transactions he was interested in earlier, were the ones made by the bulls and bears. To make a profit, James could go to any length and at times not be totally fair. He hated losing, be it on the tennis court or fighting hard in the business arena. This often led to plenty of friction between him and the rest of his team, especially earnest and honest players like Amit Vyas. Amit had been fired according to the whims and fancies of James who always had an upper hand with the senior management as he knew how to massage their egos and how to pull the strings of the people working at lower-level and mid-level management. Some couldn't win a debate with him; others didn't deem it fit to waste their time and effort in a losing battle. Amit, for instance, was hired by Gold Vest, a rival firm, which was rising chop-chop. Amit was one of the core members of the team. James' ego let him go at that moment but now he realized it was again a wrong choice or call he had made in his life. 'Amit, you were the right choice. My decision was wrong. Once I am back, I will undo what I had done', James decided.

There was something else which was back, the sunrise. The whole night, James' mind had been reeling with emotions back and forth like the pendulum of an antique clock. James knew now that he could not bring back time but he certainly could make choices that could result in storybook endings. It would mean that he would only have to write these chapters afresh and with positive intent. The sunlight reflecting on his window probably symbolized his new found upbeat mood.

He monologued, 'It's time for D-day'. No, he was not going to wage a war or attack anyone. It was time to learn the next chapter in his *ABCD* journey called *D,* for *Discipline.* He couldn't wait as he put on his jogging gear and his headphones. As he was about to take his first step outside his room, he played press on his little audio device.

The voice brought music to his ears, it was Guruji as he said, "Good morning friends, what I am about to tell you can change your life but I am not a magician or an occult Guru. Your life can only change when you make the effort. That has to come from within. For that to happen, you will have to play your intellect and emotions in sync just like in any symphony. This symphony I am about to explain to you will help you synchronize your mind, body and soul across your seven concentric layers so that your life remains in perfect rhythm like a beautiful rainbow."

James was all ready to play the game of life with utmost discipline. He began increasing his pace with every word of Guruji as his voice from the recording resounded in his ears, "Friends, life is a sport and you have to play it with utmost discipline."

A few years ago

RK *was addressing an annual day gala of his enterprise, talking emotively to his team.*

"… *Friends it was a tough choice but our leadership team and all of you made it happen. Yes, the board had me by the throat but today they are patting me on my back. I am happy it was all worthwhile.*

"*Making a choice is a step in the right direction. But is that enough? Today, we have all gathered here to celebrate the annual gala and have the fire in our bellies to achieve greatness. This choice might fizzle out tomorrow morning and we will be busy with our reports, calls and emails. And for some it might also mean the family, parties and after-parties. Yes, we will have one tonight, don't worry.*"

The audience burst out laughing.

He continued, "*What's important for us is the Discipline to realize the Choice we have made. Let us focus, as a team, to:*

- *Communicate, don't complain.*
- *Collaborate, don't control.*
- *Lead by example, don't micromanage.*
- *Prompt, don't point fingers.*

"*When you add these little things to your everyday list, they will take you a long way. Just like you have an alarm clock to wake you up in the morning. I am not talking about nocturnal party animals here.*"

Again, there was a ha-ha moment in the crowd.

"*Have an internal alarm clock to introspect and critique your own performance when things are not going your way. Like form is temporary, class is permanent, similarly, motivation is temporary, discipline is permanent.*"

CHAPTER 18
Discipline is dedication at work

D is for Discipline

James was jogging at around six miles per hour but his thoughts were running at a million miles per second. So many thoughts and people were still scuttling around in his head since last night. He was perhaps on the last stages of his coaching from Guruji but there were so many firsts he was enlightened with. As he reached the canteen of the Ashram, he met the usual familiar faces at the venue.

Dr. Mac Raj from Houston was planning to introduce spiritual sciences in the medical science curriculum in his department. Senthil Henriksen, the football coach of a leading international football club, was planning to make yoga mandatory at his club and coaching center. Then there was the corporate honcho Che Lang from Singapore who was planning to make meditation a mandatory practice at his workplace. He even met a Hollywood actor from Australia, Mark, who had worked with his Eliza in a film. Mark spoke about Eliza briefly not knowing James' equation with her in the past. For the first time, James evoked no emotions but just a sense of calm. He had begun to become more aware of his emotions, to breathe easy, and to make the right choices.

James thought such exceptional people all under the same

roof is no fluke or sham. There was a bigger force which had pulled them all to this Ashram. These top shots were now foot soldiers and torchbearers of a redefined approach to living. It was not just one day or one or two people. Day in and day out hundreds of them were doing it like a selfless mission.

"James, what's the first thing that comes to your mind when you hear the word 'discipline'?"

James' mind immediately moved back to his school days where his teachers would often shout at him or complain to his parents about his lack of discipline. He always thought that he was born with this trait. He was a rebel without a cause or direction. The only thing that worked in his favor was that he excelled in academics and sports despite his shenanigans at school.

"I can rather describe the word 'indiscipline' with me being sent to summer school during the vacations."

"Now why am I not surprised?" Guruji smiled, looking at James.

"I have plenty of episodes to share with you."

"None that I am interested in. Let me ask you a question, "What's your favorite sport?"

"I love tennis."

"What if you could beat Roger Federer in a match tomorrow, what would you call it?"

"A fluke or a miracle."

"Exactly. Miracles or flukes happen once a while. Can you win so many grand slams with flukes?"

"No way, it takes sheer hard work, diligence, motivation and determination."

"You forgot the word focus. In fact, your favorite player,

Roger Federer picked up a tennis racket when he was just eight years old."

"If you sum up all the words above, there is only one word for it."

"Discipline?"

"Yes, unfortunately, discipline, for you James and many others is external because you always think of your teachers or parents trying to discipline you. In reality, discipline is something that has to be internal. Without self-discipline, you cannot complete the ABC of life."

"I don't understand."

"James, I talked about *Awareness, Breathing* and *Choices* over the last few days. Now tell me if you don't practice this regularly, what will happen?"

"Back to square one from where I started or landed up here."

"Exactly, let's go back to tennis, what are the different kinds of shots in tennis?"

"There is serve, volley, smash and slice."

"Great, so, tell me James, can Roger Federer say I am not practicing volley and smash today? I will just serve and slice?"

"Not possible, for you to be a complete player, you need to practice all the shots in the book and even innovate some out on the court."

"Precisely James, for you to win the game of life, you need to practice the techniques of *Awareness, Breathing* and *Choices* every day without fail. Even a great player like Roger Federer cannot say he will not practice today."

"Makes total sense."

"Let me share another interesting piece of trivia with you. How many gold medals has Usain Bolt won at the Olympics and World Championships?"

"A lot, I don't know the exact number."

"He won 20 golds out of 21 races that he participated in."

"That's phenomenal!"

"Yes, it surely is but hear this out, do you know how many minutes it adds up to in total for all those gold-medal runs?"

"No idea."

"Less than 15 minutes if you add up all those seconds into minutes."

"That's it?"

"What did you expect? We are not talking about Marathons here. "Imagine those 15 minutes sum up an entire man's life and achievements. But no one sees the kind of discipline the man must have practiced every single day to reach his goal. Today, after retirement, the man is reaping the benefits of his self-discipline, right from the time he first set foot on the world stage in 2001. He must have toiled millions of minutes to date only to win in those 15 minutes. If that is not discipline James, what is?"

"My God Guruji, now that you put it that way, his feat is remarkable. We just think of the medals and not the sweat, blood and toil behind each one of them."

"Yes, people give a lot of credit to Usain Bolt's physical anatomy and toughness as an athlete. I have another example of an incredible world champion who fought internal demons after being diagnosed with a mental disorder."

"Who is that?"

"Michael Phelps, the world champion in swimming. Not many people know that Michael Phelps suffered from ADHD, a mental disorder seen in kids, which is marked by acute attention deficit and hyperactive behaviors. Children with ADHD have problems in focusing and paying attention. They often indulge in irrational impulsive behavior, which could be difficult to control. Imagine a child who cannot focus on his goals and is not aware of his true potential. Yet he goes on to become the greatest swimmer ever and one of the most decorated Olympians! Michael credits much of achievements to his limitations as a child. It helped him create records and milestones, which seem matchless at the moment. Consider this, the man has won 28 medals at the Olympics, 23 of them gold, which include 7 world records. Now that's a man who has walked or rather swam all over the competition. So, how did he do it?"

"That's a million-dollar question."

"Ever seen a shark swimming in the sea, James?"

"Oh Yes, on National Geographic, in real life and in movies."

"When a shark is in the ocean, it is perhaps one of the most feared predators. Its movements underwater is literally visual poetry in motion. It's both fluid and freaky. But when it's on land, it goes into a frenzy and loses all control. It's no more feared but becomes the hunted. Michael was extremely prankish in school with no self-control, creating hysteria in and around the campus."

"One fine day he found his playground. It was the swimming pool. A place that made him a predator who hunts his prey in the form of medals, which would motivate him one race after another. The goals and visions he couldn't see on the surface, he submerged them under the water. He found his level-playing field and another very important thing, which we all should have in life."

"What's that?"

"A mentor. No athlete or leader can become great without a mentor. History has shown us that the greatest sportsmen, rulers, statesmen and corporate leaders had mentors to whom they owe much of their success."

"That brings me to an important question Guruji."

"I am all ears."

"You said discipline is internal and not external but a coach or mentor is an external factor, then why do we need them?"

"James, excellent question. OK, let me explain it with a little example. Imagine, you are standing on the second floor of a building and watching the wonderful scene below. Suddenly, you realize there is an open drain. What's worse? There is a toddler who is playing down the road and might not be aware of the drain. The next second, you realise that the kid is in a playful mood and does not realise the danger ahead. Now, what would you do? Wait for that little toddler to make an internal or well-informed decision when it does not even know what lies ahead? I am sure you will either signal the child to stop or run down the stairs and try to get the kid out of that situation."

James looked slightly perplexed as he said, "Right, but how is that related to a coach?"

"James, coaches are the ones who spot the dangers ahead of you and help you overcome them well in time. They help you improve not just your craft or skill but also your physical and mental game. Without a coach, we would all be like that little kid meandering down the street, carefree. Without a path or vision."

"You mean putting you back on track?"

"Yes James, a coach does not discipline us but rather helps us realize our inner discipline."

James thought: yet again Guruji has simplified something that most of us find so complex in life! In his search for money, fame and power, James had forgotten to empower or inspire people. He felt as if he had let so many small children fall into the ditch when he could have stopped or warned them. 'Forget self-discipline, I was always self-centered'. That's the thought that kept playing in his mind.

"I must say I fell short in that department."

"Let me ask you another question. Do you know how many hours we sleep in our lifetime?"

"Yes, I read somewhere that it is one-third of our life."

"Yes, that's somewhere around 20 to 25 years of our life that we spend sleeping and dreaming."

"Can you guess how many years in a lifetime you use to commute, that's only work and home?"

"No Guruji, never looked at it that way."

"Let me throw some light on that. You will probably end up spending two to three years of your life just commuting."

"What a colossal waste."

"Now tell me, James, if you were to add up all the hours you would be working or rather grinding at work, do you know how many years that comes to?"

"You are asking a workaholic."

"Exactly, so do you know James?"

"No, Guruji."

"On average, 13-15 years of your life will be gone just working"

"Really?"

"If you were to spend seven hours in school every day,

that's almost 140 to 150 days every year of school. That means approximately 12,600 hours or 525 days. So nearly two years of your life go towards your schooling. Then comes college and your Master's degree. Now, James, you do the Math and yes don't forget the vacations or leave we take in a year."

"Guruji, what's the point here? Why are you telling me all this?"

"This is not what I am saying, this is what the great Muhammad Ali said in one of his famous speeches where he stressed that we have very little time on planet earth and how we need to make it productive. We have a very few years in our life to work at full-steam. So, if you want to go all-out in the race called life, *ABCD* is the best way to stay on top of the game."

"Everyone knows Lionel Messi for being a magician on the football pitch but did you know, as a kid he had growth hormone deficiency, which jeopardised not just football but his family's financial and mental health? Despite the odds, Messi had to take hundreds of these injections for a few years, which made him a footballer and, thank God, gave us the opportunity to see his artistry at work."

"Oh, I have travelled to Europe just to see Barcelona play against Real Madrid."

"So, James are you seeing a common thread in all these personalities? And I am not talking about some hashtags."

"Yes, Guruji, the one common thread between these personalities is the fact that they all had plenty of roadblocks in their life but they never stopped in their journey and used self-discipline as fuel, which kept their engines running."

"This brings me to the point, James, once you have the *ABCD* program covered, you create a system like an investment. All you have to do is put in your money. Then the money starts making more money for you."

"Hence, never forget the system of *Awareness,* which is putting your mind to the right things at the right time and the right place. *Breathing* is all about harnessing your emotions and *Choice* is all about filtering your decisions based on your awareness and breathing patterns. Once you follow this system consistently, you'll notice you will have plenty of aces as in tennis, plenty of free-kicks as in football and plenty of knock-outs as in boxing."

A Few Years ago....

RK had already cemented his position as a transformative role model CEO in the Corporate world. He was celebrated for the unprecedented turn-around of his company's fortune during the economic slowdown.

However, his announcements of giving ESOP (Employee stock option) to every employee, allocating funds for L&D (Learning & Development) and Innovation - and calling them partners-in-progress, took his persona to a totally different league.

RK received many invitations to join the boards of large business conglomerates. He joined some. The stocks of all the companies his name was associated with, zoomed overnight. He was the role-model and super rock-star of the corporate world, though he always kept himself away from the limelight and put his team first. It was this down-to-earth approach that made him different from many of his peers....

Chapter 19
ABCD? E – Experimentation next

James woke up the next morning with a burning hunger to unleash his new being. It was indeed his renaissance or an upgraded 2.0 version of him. The last few days saw him learning some incredible life lessons. He was ready to go back and face the challenges that were awaiting him. The legal tussles, the broken relationships and the leadership crisis. He was ready to face them all.

"Not so soon James. I can see the exuberance in you. You also feel that the *ABCD* knowledge you possess will ease you pains in life. Not so fast my friend."

"I am not too sure what you are talking about, Guruji."

"James having learned and upgraded yourself is not the true meaning of the *ABCD* of life. This model has to be tried and tested in the real world. Not just that, you will have to share it with others, which will empower them and create new versions of themselves."

"Guruji, I have been practicing ever since you taught me these lessons."

"James, let me guess, you must have been to a lab many times in your lifetime?"

"Not my favorite place or subject – chemistry but yes, plenty of times, you are right again."

"James, usually experiments are conducted in a controlled environment to avoid any complications or accidents. Plus, in a controlled environment, your success rate goes up and you can get seamless and uninterrupted results."

"That's right, though some experiments end up miserably," James retorted. His mind went back to the accident at Neo Industries, which had literally turned his life into a somersault just like the car he was in during the accident. Though, the best thing that had happened to him was coming to this Ashram. He still couldn't believe that this Ashram was referred to him by Dr. Riya Soni, the doctor who was treating him at the hospital after his accident. Today, medical science was heavily divided between medical elixir vs the spiritual potion of life.

Some people from the medical community think that science has all the answers to the medical problems of today while others have a much more balanced approach. They recognize that spirituality is science and not just an art form claimed as by medical pundits. Dr. Soni was one of them and due to her, James was sitting right here, right now, at the Ashram.

"James, in science you have a set of compounds or elements, which have certain properties and observations that react in a certain way. For example, water on the iron surface will result in corrosion because of pure scientific chemical reaction. Leaving the milk outside, will result in it being decomposed because of bacterial reaction in the milk. So, we have all these definitive experiments and rules in science."

"That's right but what has this got to do with the *ABCD* of life?"

"Everything James. Fortunately, or unfortunately human engineering is not an experiment to be tested in a controlled environment. This Ashram is like the lab which offers the perfect ambience to conduct experiments. But as you know, all experiments are ultimately conducted for the world, beyond the lab. Similarly, the *ABCD* of life has to be conducted outside the periphery of the Ashram. That's where you will evolve and grow as a person."

"What do you suggest, Guruji?"

"Explore. Experience. Examine. Not just the external world but the internal universe. Put on your wandering cap and see the world. Visit the length and breadth of the country. Meet people from all walks of life. Right from the fakirs to the famous."

"But India is such a vast country, where would I go?"

"That's for you to decide but covering some of the spiritual hubs of the country would be a good start. And yes, lead an ordinary life. No flights and fancy hotels. Use local transport, blend in with the people and their cultures. Mix well into the local flavours. That's how you learn the true nuances of human engineering. The whole world is an experiment, make the best of it. I wish you all the best."

"Guruji after learning so much, I suddenly feel lost, why are you deserting me?"

"On the contrary James, I am helping you find yourself. Human engineering is not about spoon feeding. There are no shortcuts. Always remember one thing James, no matter wherever you are, always remember the *ABCD*. You cannot afford to miss it even for a day. It will help you navigate through the roadblocks that come your way. Just like you have Google maps to help you find your way in the external world, *ABCD* will be the Google maps in your internal operating system to choose the right emotions and arrive at the right decisions."

The next few days James spent chalking out the various destinations in India that he wanted to visit. One on his list was the four dhams in the state of Uttarakhand, which are said to be highly auspicious as well as mystical. Next was Puri, Bodh Gaya, Dwarka and Rameswaram. Plus, he was not going to miss Varanasi and Rishikesh, which is called the Yoga capital of the world. He was also planning on going to the West, places like Ajmer and Goa.

Once the plan was in place, James was all set to pack his bags. There was more than his personal stuff that he was packing. He had to load all the learnings from the Guruji into the vehicle of his mind which travels at a limitless pace and takes one to endless places. He was already missing the moments and the people at the Ashram.

As he was leaving the Ashram that day, he felt he was, at last, arriving in life thanks to the lessons of this spiritual abode and the priceless teachings of Guru Manvik. He reached the city center bus stand. From here he was ready for the adventure and experiment called LIFE.

The next 90 days were the most grueling days of his life. From the sweat-dripping bodies to surviving on bare necessities, James had a reality-check of what billions go through on this planet to make ends meet. As he browsed through each village and town on the way, he was awe-inspired to see that spirituality played a larger role than anything else in the faith and fate of the people in this country. Right from the impoverished to the extremely prosperous, everyone was connected to divinity. Some called it religion, others called it spiritualism.

From the stimulating evergreen-laden pine trees of the Himalayan ranges to the indigo waters of the Lakshadweep down south, James had seen it all. He met the meditating Sadhus or Sages up north in the snow-clad Himalayas who wore but minimalistic clothes and seemed to be in maximum control over their mind, body and soul.

As he traversed down south, he noticed the skin tones change from lighter shades to darker hues but the hospitality was just as bright up North as down South. From being a lot richer in oil and ghee, the southern part of the country was pungency and spices galore. South India is an ancient spice trade hub, which is reflected in their food. From the thick creamy Mughlai gravies up north to the thin zesty Sambar, the food had countless textures, colours and flavors. James thought the food was definitely an incentive to stay back and get lost in the crowd of nearly 1.3 billion people. It was adding to his *ABCD* regimen, which he was following religiously.

India is not just a north-south escapade for those smitten by wanderlust. The east-west jaunt was also a long-winded feast for the wander-lusters of the world. From the glorious white sand desert at the Rann of Kutch luminescing on a full moon night to Cherrapunji in the far east and one of the mistiest places on earth, James felt wild and free like the native bird of north-east India, the Hodgson's Frogmouth.

On the way, he snaked through the by lanes of Kolkata, which teems with old-world charm and the ethos of vibrant art, culture and artifacts of the colonial era. He stopped for a *tabla* concert in the city, and then moved on to seeing an artist strum a guitar in India's rock capital – Shillong. It seemed that the whole city had a rhythm playing in the background and the people swaying to its beat on the streets. If he was grooving in one city, he was meditating in the next one which is one of the most spiritual and holiest places in India. India has given not just the science of spirituality but the art of making love, which was evident in the temples of Khajuraho in central India. James thought it was a beautiful fusion of esoteric and erotic lore.

Looking for the erstwhile, he found himself immersed in the ultra-cosmopolitan setting of Mumbai. So far, he felt the pace of India to be chilled out like a piece of slow-motion choreography. But in Mumbai, he had to quickly change the tempo of his pace. This city moves in fast forward mode. Everything just keeps zipping through the city. Right from the pedestrians on the streets to the local trains loaded with an ocean of people. No wonder it is called the 'maximum city'. It is number two on the global list as the most densely populated city in the world. From seeing the dense rainforests in the east, he was witnessing the massive concrete jungles housing millions of people in skyscrapers with the price of these abodes growing steeper with each floor and district. Through some of his old contacts, he got in touch with a dew of his corporate friends and artists in the razzmatazz world of Bollywood.

James thought the concept of unity in diversity is not just an adage in India. It exists in its natural ecosystem as well. He created a log of photos on his smartphone wherever he went. He took selfies with Sadhus and even puffed some of the finest weed with them, cooked home meals with locals at villages and travelled in the rickety buses and jaded train compartments to understand the roots of the Indian culture.

And before he realized it, he had already completed 90 days, which had been bliss for him, a hundred percent. Then he began his final journey to his favorite place from where it all began.

A few years ago...

With success comes new challenges and barriers. So, was the case with RK.

There was another big economic slowdown, and RK needed some out-of-the-box ideas and again be a game-changer for his enterprise. He went about his business in a methodical and meticulous way. A wise man had once told him, 'break the larger problem into smaller blocks and suddenly you will find micro solutions to each problem'.

First, he analyzed the markets in which a slowdown was declared. What struck him was that though there was a hullabaloo and pandemonium by the media and the so-called Business Pundits, some countries and economies were clearly not reflecting this commotion and still had GDP growth rate in the green. RK identified those markets and the sectors and decided to go Global!

He went against the tide and created expansions in those markets where there was demand. He took a big risk and offered key roles of new market development to his existing employees instead of hiring external experts. He had confidence in the potential of his team.

This decision did not go down too well with his Board of Directors who were at loggerheads with him. He assured them with a one-line brief "Just wait and watch."

He asked for a period of one year or else he would offer his resignation. Though initially his plan B looked like a C-grade idea, slowly but surely the fortunes of the company began to change. Soon both top and bottom lines showed solid growth. His company was now going places....

CHAPTER 20
A Rendezvous with Deja Vu

After 90 days of travelling, James was back at Triveni Ghat at Guruji's Ashram. He looked leaner and weaker from his travel exploits. He narrated his stories about his mystical encounters with the Sages to flirty conversations with starlets from Bollywood. One of the disciples asked him a question.

"So, James which city gave you the goosebumps."

"I think that's not a fair question for a country that stretches more than 3 million kilometers with an unmatched diversity. Let me say, every city has its own inexplicable charm but there was one city I did connect to, for some unfathomable reason. Any guesses?"

"Was it Mumbai?"

"I bet it was Goa!"

"Delhi it must have been for its food and culture."

Numerous answers came from the crowd and finally Guruji looked at him and said, "Bodh Gaya".

James was speechless. He could not fathom how Guruji got it right even when he had not shared his entire itinerary with him.

"Am I right James?"

James looked at him and saluted him like an army man.

"How did you know?"

"It's simple James, the spark in your eyes and the fluency in your thoughts and actions tell me that you are enlightened just like another man was 2000 years ago. His name is Gautam Buddha."

"That's right, what is even more interesting is the fact that I felt as if I had been to this place even though I was visiting it for the first time. I felt as though I had been part of the local dialect, those alluring streets and meditative culture. How's that even possible?"

"James ever heard about Déjà vu?"

"Yes, though I never did understand the art or science behind it."

"Ok, can you recall any of your Déjà vu moments?"

"It was one time when I made a huge gamble on a small company's stocks and it paid off big time by the end of the day. The fact is that I felt I had already seen this stock make huge profits and I had been celebrating that success with my company CEO."

"Great example James. I am sure when your thoughts visualized that event, your emotions in that present moment were giving you some inexplicable signals about the future. That very moment is called Déjà vu."

"I like where you are going but can you simplify this further?"

"Déjà vu is a French word which literary means 'already seen' or in other words it means 'reliving a past moment'. This happens to most people in their lifetime, and is associated with experiential feeling because you feel something of the past in the present moment, which has never happened!"

"Guruji, so why do I feel a bit different in those Déjà vu moments? Not sure if I am able to articulate...but the feeling in those moments is beyond words and explanation. Is there any logic or science behind it?"

"Yes, there is."

"See, in these moments, your Awareness is fully focused on observing your Emotions of that present moment!"

"That's like a hell of a statement – what does it mean?"

"Ok, I will explain it again with a slightly different approach."

"See, a human mind continuously oscillates between the thoughts and feelings of past, present and future. You agree?"

"Yes, I do – this happens with me and with everyone, all the time, but so what?"

"It's not 'so what'? It's the only key to the locker called mind!"

"Meaning?"

"When your Awareness is fully focused upon observing your Emotions of that present moment – the mind does not oscillate in past and future with any other thought or feeling. It just remains there in that present moment."

"This is the moment where past-present-future merge, and everything just becomes the present moment – the oscillatory pendulum of the mind stops in that present moment. The mind just wants to experience the emotions of that present moment – that is why it is beyond words or explanation but only something to be experienced!"

"That's spot on, and makes complete sense – wow, too good!"

James went into monologue – 'Déjà vu, I understood you today'.

He certainly had picked up something new from Experimentation after learning *ABCD*.

"James, have you heard of Nikola Tesla?"

"Are you asking me about the famous scientist and futurist of the 20th century?"

"Yes."

"Of course, I have heard about him but why bring up his name in a Déjà vu conversation?"

"For a reason. One of his popular discoveries was that everything in this universe is energy which vibrates at a certain frequency. This is extremely relatable in our daily lives. Imagine you walk into a party where you don't know anyone. Have you noticed that right from the time you enter the party till the time you leave, you only connect and network with a few while the rest ignore you or vice versa? That's not all, you even believe that you have met these people before or have seen them somewhere. Now why does this happen? Think about it, when you entered you didn't know anyone but then, in an instant, you even started believing that you have met some of these people or that you had been to that place before. You ignore it as a coincidence, but should you?"

"What else could it be if not mere coincidence?" James inquisitively asked.

"Go a step further. As per Tesla's theory, each human represents energy which vibrates at a certain frequency. Let me give you an analogy - when you try to tune into an FM station, you have to scan through to certain frequencies before you can listen to your favorite songs or channels. Isn't it?"

"Yes. So?"

"This is exactly what happens when you meet people at a party. Every individual represents Energy, which is vibrating at a certain frequency. When your vibration and frequency signals match someone, you connect with that person. What's more? There is a strange feeling sometimes, when you meet a person for the first time you feel as if you had met that person before. This is Déjà vu. It brings your past, present and future on the same plateau leaving you ecstatic.

"When you visited Bodh Gaya, your frequency and vibrations were resonating with the people and surroundings there. That is why you had a Déjà vu moment in Bodh Gaya."

James was stunned. Till then Déjà vu had meant mere serendipity to him. Not any more...

A few years ago...

Several case-studies were published in all the leading magazines and business journals about RK's sharp business acumen and X-Factor to push businesses ahead and pull people along with them.

One morning each employee had an envelope on their desks with their names inscribed in gold. When they opened it, they found a few golden words from their chief in command – RK.

"Ladies and Gentleman, a year ago when I took some business decisions, many thought that I was on the path of derailment for myself and the company. But I always had a vision for our company – to create a timeless entity, evolving with changeless core values and growing it to infinity.

"A big thank you for having had faith in me as your captain. The heights and glory we have achieved as an organization is only because of great team spirit hence each one of you deserve the accolades and the credit.

"And like all journeys end, so has mine. After giving it my all, I have decided to step down from the position of CEO as I need to take a sabbatical to focus on my next adventure. Life's all about moving from one adventure to the next. Each one of us have to discover it. I have found mine knocking right at my door. What about you?"

CHAPTER 21
Human Engineering is the Dance of Rhythm and Melody

"James, there is someone here to see you," Guruji said.

"James come back to me; I miss you." Eliza was standing right in front of him.

"James, we need you back at Neo." It was Matt standing next to Eliza.

"James, we are right behind you." JJ was there too, right next to the others.

James couldn't believe his eyes. How did they know that he was here at the Ashram? He was shell shocked and did not know how to react.

"How did you find me?" He was surprised and more elated than dejected.

"How, where and what, all these questions can be answered later, James. What's important is for you to come back to us. Guruji has told us everything about you and we think that this is the right time."

Eliza moved closer to him, "Yes, James. We all make mistakes. There's no point in running away from them. Embrace them, we are all with you." She placed a hand on his shoulder, which caught him napping. Yes, he was napping.

This was just a dream. A beautiful one though. 'Alas, if only it were true,' James thought whimsically.

In reality, there was someone who had placed his hand on his shoulder. It was Guruji.

"Had a dream James? I imagine it was a good one as I see those shimmering eyes yearning to go back home."

"Maybe that was a Déjà vu moment for something that could happen in the future."

"James, it's a brand-new day, do you see the sunrise out there in all its glory?"

"Yes, it's a gift to mankind which nature offers every day and yet we use, abuse and take it for granted."

"You couldn't have put it better James. Your perspective is shining bright like the sunlight on the horizon. This brings me to a very important ingredient of human engineering and architecture. It's rather the architecture of nature, which affects human engineering at every level. James, people say the fire was what sparked human evolution. I agree but do you know what gave it the impetus?"

"The wheel?"

"Exactly. It put everything in motion or rather a revolution. It created a whole cycle of civilization, development and evolution. Everything is designed to run in a cycle. That sunrise will turn into a sunset in the next twelve hours. The summer turns from autumn to winter to spring and finally back to summer. This happens in the macro-cosmic layer of nature. And it happens in the micro-cosmic layer too. Do you know what the micro-cosmic layer is?"

"No, have not given it a thought."

"It's early morning, tell me, how do you feel this morning?"

"I feel as fresh as a daisy. All ready to go and embrace

life."

"I am glad to hear that. You gave me two keywords. 'Fresh' and 'daisy'."

"Now tell me, when I say the word 'night', what comes to your mind?"

"Nippy, indoors and sleep".

"Excellent, now you gave me three keywords."

"Guruji, please could you elaborate?"

"James the answer lies in your keywords. When you said daisy and fresh, what season would you associate it with?"

"Spring"

"And when you said nippy, indoors and..." Even before Guruji finished James replied, "Winter".

"See, there you go. Now you are getting the hang of it."

"Morning symbolizes spring. Afternoon resembles summer. Evening signifies autumn and night stands for winter. This is the cycle of nature at the micro-cosmic level every 24 hours. The keyword here is the 'cycle'."

"So true, so simple and yet so structured, nature has designed everything with a meaning."

"Let's move further - remember, we humans had a barter system before the invention of currency and organized money. Well, guess what? Nature has had a barter system with us for thousands of years."

"What do you mean?"

"James look closely, we need oxygen, which is prepared by the vegetation around us and we produce carbon dioxide, which is the main input for flora around us. Without this cycle, any life, evolution or civilization would have been impossible."

"Wow, so true – this phenomenon is also cyclic, similar to

four seasons or sunrise-sunset!"

"What's sad is that we are destroying this cycle thanks to far fewer trees than before and far more carbon emissions by the day. It won't be long before the cycle will have a puncture and we will hit a roadblock. We are adding more environmental junk to our nature, which is leading to global warming and the Intensive Care Unit (ICU) for the human race in a few years, unless we act now."

"Yes, Guruji. It surely is sad."

"James the bottom line is that change is the only constant. Your feelings and thoughts also go through a makeover all the time."

"Take, for example, your first crush in college. In hindsight, you must feel that you were naive or stupid doing things for her. You cannot be blamed for it. You were a different being then. Young blood and pumping testosterone can be a lethal mix sometimes."

James thought back on his first crush, Jennifer in his college, for whom he would do anything. Right from college notes to holding an umbrella for her in the rain, he had it all covered. And how did she reciprocate? She introduced him to every new boyfriend of hers and ran away to California for an acting career. Today, she was dancing to the tunes of her three kids and her ex-husband who was finalizing their divorce.

"I am sure you could have a good laugh when you look back to those memories."

"You bet Guruji, I am laughing."

"See, you didn't look like this 20 years ago and you won't be in this shape for another 20 years. Similarly, your intellect changes over time as you are faced with new emotions and perceptions. "You might not share the same bond with the friends of your college days because you have moved on or maybe they have. On the other hand, there might be some friends with whom you haven't talked for years but when you do, it feels just like yesterday. Life's like an ever-swinging pendulum of emotions and decisions, which either add momentum to your life or decelerates it, till your last breath."

"But as per the law of Physics, a change can only be recognized with reference to a changeless entity. For example, the movement of a bus or car is noticeable with reference to the static objects outside. However, movement of an aircraft is not noticeable as there isn't anything in a cloudless sky to relate it to."

"That's so true!"

"Therefore, for recognizing the changes in your personality and their functions postulate the existence of an unchanging entity in you, isn't it?"

James had his eyes now fixated at that moment.

"Before I move forward if I were to ask you to describe yourself in a paragraph, how would you do it?"

"Hi, my name is James Hatman. I am an investment banker by profession but an auto-enthusiast by passion. I have a penchant for taking road trips with the latest bikes and cars around the world. My favorite sports are tennis and football. My life's greatest revelation has been the awe-inspiring human engineering and *ABCD* program designed at this Ashram. My body, mind, intellect, memory and ego have been upgraded with this unique program. I don't want to talk about my older version anymore because this is the new me, version 2.0 and raring to go."

"Wonderful, what was the keyword in what you just told

me?"

"When you talk about key, I can only think of car keys." They both had a nice chuckle.

"Yes, I can see your passion for cars and speed."

"The keyword here is My".

"So, how is it important in human engineering?"

"In English, the use of the possessive pronoun *my* indicates that there are two entities, the possessor and the possessed. The word *my* makes you the possessor."

"And whatever you are describing by using the word *'my'* i.e. the body, mind, intellect, memory, ego - they are your possessions, isn't it?"

James was hearing something very profound, again for the first time in his life.

"This is a bit complex, but can you see the point James?"

"Yes, I do."

"Great!"

"Now, if I take away the possessed entities i.e. body-mind-intellect-memory-ego, then what is left?"

"Nothing."

"But a minute ago you said - '*My* body, mind, intellect, memory and ego have been upgraded with this unique *ABCD* program'. Isn't it?"

James was zapped at the very thought.

"I don't know — I would just be a cypher or a non-entity."

"Well James, but you still feel that there is something which integrates these faculties — body, mind, intellect, memory, ego and claim them as its possessions. Isn't it?"

"Ya, that's true," a perplexed James muttered.

"If you take away all, then nothing is left, yet there is something which treats them as *my* possessions. Correct?"

James' mind came racing back. "So, what is that?"

"James, that unseen and unknown entity is called the *Atman,* the *Soul* within. This is present as the seventh layer, the core of the seven concentric layers of human engineering. This is the timeless-changeless entity which manifests via *Kernel* to all layers; and also permeates across all dimensions, life after life."

James was sitting speechless and mesmerized while there was glee on Guruji's face.

"As this timeless-changeless layer permeates through the seed layer *kernel,* it forms the beautiful rainbow of the seven concentric layers of the human personality."

"Do you remember the seven layers of the rainbow?"

James could clearly visualize the seven-concentric layer rainbow chart in front of his eyes.

'That's so real and logical', he went into his monologue

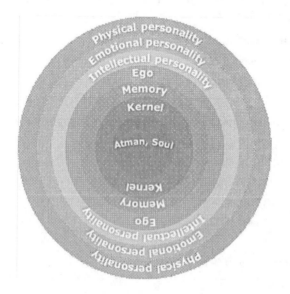

mode.

"Just close your eyes for 30 seconds James, and imagine this perfect harmony of human engineering."

James closed his eyes and was imagining the beauty of the rainbow colours across the seven concentric layers of human engineering. He was amazed at the potent and seamless combination of science and philosophy.

He was now able to correlate the relevance of the *ABCD* regime across these seven layers. He had never imagined that there is engineering behind everything, even when it comes to our emotions. It was an awesome moment for him!

"With consistent practice of *ABCD* you will soon be able to achieve maximum mileage for your personality-vehicle. This module will help you achieve quicker pit stops, maximum efficiency and the right gears to steer you out of problems and offer you pole positions in life. It just needs the right balance to get those wheels revving optimally per second."

James was hearing for the first time, a scientific equation to life. He said, "You know how much I love cars and that's why you are giving me these examples."

"Well, you may interpret it that way James. Working regularly on this translates to better thoughts, emotions and actions for you. And when that happens, it brings a shift in perception of present moments."

"This is an *Experiential* phenomenon no words can explain. It can only be felt. This is a paranormal phenomenon beyond the realms of terrestrial science." And when this orchestra runs in symphony, you are in sync with your inner and outer world – you arrive in Life!

"You attain:

"Peace and joy – Inside

Efficiency and dynamism – Outside"

"Simply wow!" said James Hatman.

Right from the time James had walked into the Ashram, it all started to converge.

His cycle of life was about to change....

A few years ago...

Ram Khilawan, RK was in the news across the entire corporate world. His stunning decision to suddenly step down as CEO was incomprehensable. The employees still felt that this was just a prank.

No one could understand why a man at the peak of his career would suddenly call it a day. No one knew where and when he would land up in a new venture.

Only RK knew where he was headed after he had received a letter a few days ago. A line that changed his life and destination forever. He was on a 16-hour flight from New York to New Delhi...

CHAPTER 22
Hatman meets Atman

James was all set to fly from New Delhi to New York. The number of hours he would take to reach there – 16 hours. The distance – almost 12,000 km. The thoughts running in his mind – more than a million. But this was a new James. Not the one who was an escapist filled with guilt, angst and fear running riot in his mind. Here he was all set to embrace whatever came his way. Thanks to the teachings of Guruji, he knew what emotions to keep and what to let go. He had also learned to choose the right decisions to make.

He had made a complete plan in his diary to begin his upgraded version. He played the spiritual music which had been personally given to him by Guruji. He switched on the headphones, another gift from the Guruji. Guruji had told him: 'when in doubt or despair just put these on to your ears to refresh your mind, body and soul'. The rhythmic music and soulful hymns were in perfect synchrony to put every nerve of his at ease.

At nearly 35,000 feet, his mind was in cruise control. Gone were the days of his self-indulgence. James had taken an economy class flight. He chatted with his fellow passengers. He laughed with a few and cried with one particular passenger - an 8-year-old who was flying to the US for her leukemia treatment. Guruji had once told him, 'life is an offer that should be invested well because others are not as fortunate as you are'.

Well, this girl was a living proof of it. Her smile inspired him to take life with a pinch of salt and add his own flavors to make it relishing. One point on his agenda was to create a difference for others around him. He had decided to launch a program called 'investment for humanity'. Seeing her parents also made him yearn for companionship. Eliza came rushing to his mind. He was afraid that she was long gone from his life.

An announcement came from the captain after nearly 15 hours. Just what he had been waiting for. As the captain announced that the plane would land in the next 30 minutes, his mind began to take off about the emotions, thoughts and feelings he would experience once he landed. The plane was getting ready to land and he was getting all set to arrive on the big stage – The Big Apple. The moment finally arrived when the wheels of the plane touched down and he inhaled deeply. He could smell America in the air and with great anticipation he said – 'America, I am home'.

The doors of the aircraft opened and he made his way out of the airport. What he encountered next was a sight he wouldn't forget for the rest of his life.

"James it's good to see you back, I missed you." Eliza was standing right in front of him.

"James, we need you back at Neo." It was Matt standing next to Eliza.

"James, we are right behind you," JJ was there too, right next to the rest.

It was exactly as he had dreamed a few days ago, a Déjà

vu moment. He had a smile on his face as he felt the three more sets of arms to his physical body and more importantly three more minds to his psychological personality. The Déjà vu moment meant that he now was completely aware of his thoughts, actions and feelings. The infinity was connecting to him right now. It was a propitious sign, or was it?

The next thing he encountered was the agents from the Department of Treasury who came up to him and said, "James, you have been cleared of all the charges pending against you. We just wanted to give you a heads up as soon as you landed."

JJ came up to him and said, "Neo Industries has dropped all charges against you."

"How is that even possible JJ?" an incredulous James questioned.

"I will explain everything to you once we are in the car."

As they sat in the car and coursed through the maddening traffic of Manhattan, James looked at the streets teeming with people making their way to earn a living. He used to be one of them every morning until he reached the Ashram and learnt how to live. Right now, along with the car, his wheels of fortune were turning.

"James, there were defects in the car." JJ then began telling him the story of how the Quality Control team at Neo Industries had vacillated before they let James drive that car. It was not certified as safe to even test drive and yet someone had okayed it on the day of the accident. The events that unfolded were not due to James' negligence but several mechanical failures, which were not detected nor tested beforehand.

The media circles were now calling it as 'corporate

espionage' where someone wanted to destroy James and the brand of his enterprise. Investigations were taking place as they spoke. Thanks to JJ who headed the investigation and defense, they ensured a fool-proof defense plan to protect James from this tragedy.

Suddenly, there was a lambency running through his mind which was reflected on his face with a smile. He knew if this car accident had never happened, he wouldn't have had the most remarkable accident of his entire life – the teachings of Guruji. He would still be his old self and probably irreparable.

James thought to himself, 'Guruji, I guess Déjà vu is working'.

JJ updated him with all the happenings of the company while he had been away. He explained how performance in the company had deteriorated over the last six to eight months. Staff morale was down though many of them were happy James was away because, according to them, James had zero management skills. James was objective and knew he had had many flaws. He wanted to work on them. He listened patiently to JJ who was more than just his legal advisor. He was a personal friend and confidante who had saved James many times from personal or professional disasters.

However, things were very different this time. It was a revelation to see the body language of James. He was like a cool slush of ice on a hot summer day. Melting slowly but gracefully with colours and flavors of calmness. He heard JJ with a cool head on his shoulders. In the past, he would get irritated and throw a slew of verbal volleys. Right now, he was like a sponge absorbing what came his way.

He said, "JJ I know I have screwed up things big time in the past and I cannot reverse them nor go back in time but I can certainly undo the mistakes I have made with people or situations."

This openness in his thoughts was complemented by the lush green environs of the countryside they were passing through. The concrete jungle had made way for the large expanse of fields and waterfronts on the outskirts of the city. They were on their way to Mystic, a small quaint village which had, over the years, become very popular. It was about a two-hour drive from New York and was mystic, quite literally. From sky-blue sea waters on one side and the flow of arts into the city corners, this place had something for every seeker.

"JJ what are we doing here?" He had stopped over at a house overlooking the seaport. The house was a lavish 5-bedroom bungalow with a beautiful front porch and an expansive backyard, which overlooked the blue sky that was meeting the azure colours of the water seamlessly.

As he entered, he was surprised to see the entire home themed like a spiritual center. The interiors were all white, minimalistic and had a positive aura. Suddenly something caught his eye, which completed the house and made it home. A photo of him and Eliza framed neatly, hanging on the wall. They looked so happy together. Suddenly, two hands embraced him with a peck on his lips. It was Eliza as she said, "James, this is how I see it for us from this very moment on. This is my gift to us. Remember the Australian guy Mark whom you had met at the Ashram and who had worked with me in Hollywood? He told me about you when he came back from the Ashram. He told me how you had reformed your life. We all make mistakes, maybe I intruded into your professional and personal space and blurred the lines."

"Don't belittle yourself, Eliza, if there is anyone to blame for the failure of our relationship, it was me. Not a day went by when I didn't want to say sorry to you but I also needed this time and space for something more substantial rather than something as superficial as a lame 'sorry'."

"I know it's more important to love yourself before you can commit to anyone", said Eliza. Those words took him back to one of the teachings of Guruji when he spoke about awareness.

"This is just part of the surprise; wait till I show you something else."

They walked for five minutes, hand-in-hand till she asked him to close his eyes and then turn around. He obliged. Then she told him to open his eyes. He saw a cloud of a white building with the signage – *The Atman Renaissance Hub*. Eliza was ecstatic as she said, *'Hatman meets Atman'*.

James' mind immediately went back to the 31 constituents and seven concentric layers of human engineering and how Guruji had told him about the changeless entity in us being the *Atman*. He murmured, "I guess this is the perfect name for this hub." James thought how strange it was that he had never seen this link between Hatman and *Atman* but now that he had seen it, the name was perfect. He wanted this to remain as the changeless entity long after he was gone.

This Renaissance hub would be the nucleus or as how Guruji would say, the *kernel* of wellness and inner transformation for the ever-changing external transformation of the world. This one-of-a-kind center would comprise spiritual sciences, yogic art, naturopathy and meditation techniques. The infrastructure was seamless and the location couldn't have been more perfect.

The soothing breeze of the waterfront, the languid lifestyle and its unique location in the Mystic village made the tiredness of the sixteen hour long flight, and the two hour drive from the hustle and bustle of New York, melt away in no time. James felt another Déjà vu moment standing there with plenty of goosebumps. He again felt that he had seen this place or had been here before.

He looked at Eliza and kissed her deeply. It was a kiss that awoke all seven of his concentric layers with perfect rainbow colours. What followed was a chain of events that led to the awareness of his emotions and making the right choice as he went down on his knee and popped the question: "Eliza, will you marry me?" She couldn't say 'No'.

Once his emotions were in place, it was time to make some tough choices and right decisions now that he was back. The next week he was back in the thick of action, stirring and shaking Wall Street in downtown New York. As he entered the office once again, people got up from their seats and began to clap. It's strange how he was the most hated man a few months ago but now respect was all that people had for him. He was back in the NOW. He had called for a press conference. He was about to announce a bunch of measures for the company's Renaissance now that he had seen his Renaissance center.

He came on the stage and spoke, "Today is a big day for me. I would like to begin by saying I am sorry to all my friends in the corporate and media circles for being a badass, troublemaker, thick-skinned and a rebel. I also know the kind of comments I received from you all behind my back, but they weren't entirely wrong. Thank you, those compliments were well taken, thank you."

The media had a good laugh.

"What's more important is to forget the past. We should appreciate the present and be ready to embrace the future because the *now* is in your control and the *future* is for you to shape. I feel, in our thirst for one-upmanship in the corporate world we all have forgotten how to live. Yes, I too was guilty of this. Not anymore. That is why I am announcing a set of new measures for the workforce.

- A new performance review system based on personality and not just performance.
- A personal development and wellness hub for the entire staff.
- Flexi-work timings for all employees regardless of their seniority.
- Six months of mandatory maternity leave.
- Monthly team meetups sponsored by the Friends.

"Decisions cannot be made in some corner offices. A company grows from its core and not from decisions made by a few people. Hereon, we will have an open culture with an overhaul of our physical space. We need to break down barriers and build bridges of communication. We are working for 60 to 70 hours, 5 days a week, for what? Making money for our loved ones. In the process we are losing out on a very important transaction or currency – Time. Are you making enough of it along with your money? The answer is no.

"We want to crash on the weekends or laze on our couches thanks to the entire barrage of deadlines on weekdays. I am hereby announcing that no one on my team will work more than 40 to 45 hours a week. Plus, there will be a mental coach onsite for people undergoing any psychological or emotional stress.

"Coming to the subject of our families, soon we will formulate and announce several medical and family policies for the benefit of all our employees. After all, we all have different designations at our workplaces, but at home, we have only one designation – family - and believe me no feeling or designation comes anywhere close. The success of a family is the greatest perk for you, me and everyone watching this.

"I am not doing this just for ourselves or our employees. No, it's for the environment as well. It's quite obvious that the picture is getting gloomier and scarier by the day with our carbon footprints and greenhouse emissions all going haywire. We are so busy making the green in our salary slips that we have forgotten the true greens and fruits of nature.

"I ask all leadership teams in the corporate arena today, 'how long are we going to build enterprises by slaughtering Mother Nature'? Let's stop making excuses that everything we are doing is for the growth and evolution of mankind. There won't be any evolution or humankind left once the natural world is gone. Do we want to put our balance sheet bottom lines in green while the environment goes all red? I am making a start here. The first step is that there will be no plastic allowed on the premises of Fintastic Investments from now on.

"Not just that, Neo Industries is on a clean drive too, quite literally! That's why we are announcing a zero-emissions car in the coming year. I assure you there will be zero emissions and zero accidents this time. Yes, this is the Neo or new way of doing business. For far too long, I have thought only about my own goals, designation and corner office. It's time for me to show the same passion for everything around me. From now on, we are not just going to experience growth but experiment with it too. Our evolution was an experiment, wasn't it?

"There were a lot of failed ones but the few and far between have been successful, which helped us get to where we are. We are not looking for a workforce but people who can deliver at work with force, foresight and a forthright thought process. We don't want doers. We want people who love what they do. That's because when you find your passion, you can accomplish perfection."

This was just the opening spiel of a speech that was seen by millions across the globe. For the next 30 minutes, James Hatman became a sensation on social media. Several streams were trending all over the internet like #HatmanForPresident. These were the same netizens who only a few months ago had written stuff like #JamesStopHiding or #WhereAreYouJamesHatman. It shows how the digital world can be merciless one minute and forgiving the very next.

His speech went viral and within just one day James had over 10 million hits. The Board met within a few days and thought it would be foolish not to promote James right to the top. Seeing his vision and the public response, he was invited to become CEO. When he received this news he thought, 'life has come full circle'. That's when he remembered Guruji's teachings about the changeless entity where everything right from the macro-cosmic layer to the smallest known particle of mankind is part of a cycle.

Thinking of Guruji, he remembered his words again, "James, I am handing you this envelope. Open it on the day you feel you have arrived in life, which I can say is not far away." Another of his masterstroke prognosis, which happened to be true.

For all these months, James had kept the envelope stashed away in the private locker of his office. He thought now is the moment to open the envelope and see what it was the Guruji had in store for him. He opened the envelope and the missive he began to read made his eyes open wider and wider with every word.

Guruji's letter to James:

<u>TAT TVAM ASI</u>

My dear James,

The day, when you are reading this letter, your external and internal worlds will be in harmony, performing the tango.

This is the day when I can say – 'James Hatman meets Atman'.

Tat Tvam Asi is one of the supreme declarations of Vedic science in the Sanskrit language, translated as 'That thou art' - meaning You are that, or That you are, referring to the congruence of the inner and outer world with God.

James, do you remember that you had asked me what I had done when I had completed my time learning from Guru Shiv Hari? Did I return to the corporate world or stay back to a life of renouncement or retirement in this Ashram? I told you that day, every chapter in life has a meaning and needs to open at the right time. That time has come now.

Yes, I left the Ashram and returned to the corporate world as RK, the CEO of Robo Kinetics. I faced the same challenges, fought the same battles, both internal and external and came out on top, with ABCD. Does the name RK, sound familiar to you?

Now, that you have achieved today what you aspired for; I wish you the very best in this journey.

And here's another revelation, Doctor Riya Soni happens to be my close relative. Remember, she was the last person you met in New York. She made all your travel arrangements in a jiffy. But, don't worry, she never told me what actually happened to you. She only gave me a one-line brief: 'My client has landed in a mess and I want you to give him wings to fly again'. And today, a New You is taking off again in New York.

Serve your true purpose James. Don't just make a living - live the life too. And stick to the consistent practice of ABCD, it will take your 31/7 personality rainbow to a newer odyssey.

You have the potential to be the next RK. And that's coming to you from RK himself!

Truly yours
RK...

James was speechless as though a bullet had just struck him. He read the letter again and again. He couldn't believe that the man he had been with all this while at the Ashram was the role model for millions in the corporate world. Till today, people refer to him in business case studies. How he turned around the fortune of enterprises and businesses with his sharp aptitude, insightful acumen and down-to-earth attitude was a subject for study. RK had been so low key that the most informed people wouldn't know sometimes that they were sitting beside him on a plane or at the cinemas. He kept himself away from any media glare or public stares.

Guruji – RK had once told him at the Ashram, "the greats in human history like Mahatma Gandhi, Isaac Newton or Albert Einstein did not require day-to-day hashtags like #NonviolenceforFreedom, #GravitySolved, #Theoryofrelativityfound."

James could now relate to every word Guruji had said and knew what his role was going to be from now on. That is to be a soldier amongst many, to re-engineer lives around the world.

On the other side of the world, Guru Manvik had just heard the news about James becoming the CEO. His face broke into a joyful smile.

Suddenly his eyes moved across the room. A man had just entered his room and said, "Guruji, now that we have learnt about Awareness, could we move on to Breathing?"

Guruji smiled. Another James was on his journey of transformation ....

The Recap

1. Seven concentric layers

For the basis of human engineering one needs to understand these layers, as it is the foundation to *ABCD*.

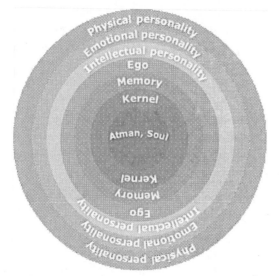

2. Awareness

Awareness is not a thing; it is background to the things that happen across human concentric layers.

Awareness exists in every human from birth. The key is 'how to raise and strengthen the awareness level'. It's like a sport where, the more you practice, the better you get at it.

<u>Strengthening awareness:</u>

finger-wonder exercise:

1. Place your index finger in front of your eyes between the centre of the eyeballs above the nose.
2. Focus on it for the 30 seconds.
3. Repeat 1, but now focus on the background, not on the finger.

   This exercise helps in strengthening awareness. When you focus on the index finger, you become aware of things in the foreground, everything else gets into blur mode. When you focus on the background, except for the background everything else gets into blur mode.

   The phenomenon is akin to the portrait mode on a smartphone.

<u>Raising awareness:</u>

Introspection & Imagination (I&I)

1. *Introspect* and become aware of the various activities which happened throughout the day - good, bad or ugly.
2. Rewind the day like a movie playing in your head without being judgemental.
   a. Don't ask *'why it is happening'* just focus on *'what is happening'*.
3. Repeat it few times, till your mind calms down.
4. Now, *imagine* if the same situation arises the next time, *how* would you tackle it differently.
   a. Just become aware of *'how' you will deal with it*. Don't question *'what' or 'why' it happened.*
5. This exercise should be done at the end of the day when going to bed, and first thing in the morning post wake up.

a. The mind stores the pictures as repository, to work on it overnight.

b. The mind is highly receptive and fresh in the morning.

3. Breathing

Breathing is the only voluntary function that can alter and transform your involuntary, autonomic nervous system. Breathing exercises raise emotional endurance levels.

Four-mula

- Four-squared is for calming.
  - o Breathe in with the count of 4
  - o Hold on to your breath for 4 seconds
  - o Exhale with the count of 4
  - o Hold on for 4 seconds before you inhale again.

To start with, do this exercise for 4 mins for the first few days, and then increase it gradually as you practice.

- Fourtify is for activating.
  - o Perform the long inhale-exhale breaths four times
  - o Exhale 40 times hard and fast through your belly
  - o Again perform the long inhale-exhale breaths four times.
  - o Exhale 40 times hard and fast through your belly

Repeat this cycle. To start with, do this for four minutes at a time for the initial few days, and then increase it gradually as you practice, going up to 14 minutes. This exercise should be done on an empty stomach or with a gap of at least two hours after eating.

4. Choices

In the principle of Cause and Effect, Choice is the Cause.

Choice is the boon endowed only to humans, but many consider it a bane.

Kernel, the seed layer is unique in every human being. It is the source which manifests as thoughts and desires at the intellectual and emotional layers respectively, and further translates as actions at the physical layer. That is why, two siblings in a family can grow up to follow two distinctly different paths. One as a police officer and the other as a dacoit or terrorist.

It's *Kernel,* the seed layer, which is responsible for you to make your choices in life. However, no matter how your seed layer kernel is, there is always a chance of reprogramming it. Only humans have been endowed with this free will of Choice.

Animals and all other living species have to live their life in a defined pre-programmed way. They do not have the free will of Choice as humans do.

5. Discipline

With consistency of *Discipline,* you strengthen *ABC.* *Awareness* puts your mind to the right things at the right time and the right place. *Breathing* helps you harness your emotions and *Choices* is all about filtering your decisions based on your awareness and breathing patterns.

Without Discipline, you cannot complete the *ABC* of life.

6. Déjà vu

Déjà vu occurrence is the feeling that you are experiencing a situation that you've been through before. It brings your past, present and future to the same plateau, leaving you ecstatic. This state brings your emotions and decisions to perfect equilibrium. The more Déjà vu moments you experience in life, the more you will be at peace with your feelings, rationale and people around you.

About the Author

An accomplished business leader, a trusted advisor, and frequent keynote speaker at various forums, Manoj Gupta has vast International experience in multiple domains. He is working in tech sector for over 25 years. His passion to innovative has helped to turn around several businesses across the world.

His approach to coalesce technology with philosophy led him towards the path of discovering intricacies of human engineering. Exploring deep into the topic by going through many books, ancient scriptures, and their interpretation by scholars and philosophers - combined with research of over 10 years, he discovered the beautiful convergence of science and metaphysics.

His fascination for human psychology and subtle difference between *'making a living'* vs *'living a life'*, inspired him to write down his idea about *'New You'*, which later became a full-fledged book. His pragmatic approach to make things simple, has motivated many people to re-evaluate their lives.

Manoj enjoys helping people and businesses to realize their true potential. He is currently working as Managing Director at Qualitest Group.